RETURN OF THE JEDI
SKETCHBOOK

RETURN OF

THE JEDI SKETCHBOOK

By Joe Johnston and Nilo Rodis-Jamero

With additional material by
Ralph McQuarrie and Norman Reynolds

Ballantine Books * New York

Artist Credits

Joe Johnston: 13, 18, 19, 22, 24, 27 (right), 28, 29, 30 (top), 32, 33, 41–46, 54–61, 65–69, 70 (bottom), 73, 75 (bottom), 77–83, 86–89, 92–96

Nilo Rodis-Jamero: 10, 14, 20, 21, 25, 37–40, 48–53, 62–64, 72, 75 (top), 90, 91

Norman Reynolds: 26 (bottom), 30 (bottom two), 31, 34 (bottom), 35, 70 (top), 71, 76, 84, 85

Ralph McQuarrie: 9, 11, 12, 16, 17, 23, 26 (top two), 27 (left), 34 (top two), 36, 47, 74

Phil Tippett: 15

Copyright © 1983 Lucasfilm Ltd. (LFL)
TM: A Trademark of Lucasfilm Ltd.

Book design by Alex Jay/Studio J

All rights reserved under International and Pan-American Copyright Conventions. Published in the United States by Ballantine Books, a division of Random House, Inc., New York, and simultaneously in Canada by Random House of Canada Limited, Toronto.

Library of Congress Catalog Card Number: 82-90903

ISBN 0-345-30959-6

Manufactured in the United States of America
First Edition: June 1983

10 9 8 7 6 5 4 3 2 1

Contents

Introduction 7

TATOOINE
Jabba the Hutt 10
Gamorrean Guards 16
The Rancor 22
The Skiff and Jabba's Sail Barge 27

ENDOR
Ewoks 36
Flying Ewoks 44
Speeder Bikes 47
Imperial Scouts 62

THE DEATH STAR
The Death Star: Unfinished Exterior 66
The Shuttle 71
The Throne Room: Interior, Death Star 76

REBEL SPACECRAFT
Rebel Cruisers 88
A-wing and B-wing Fighters 92

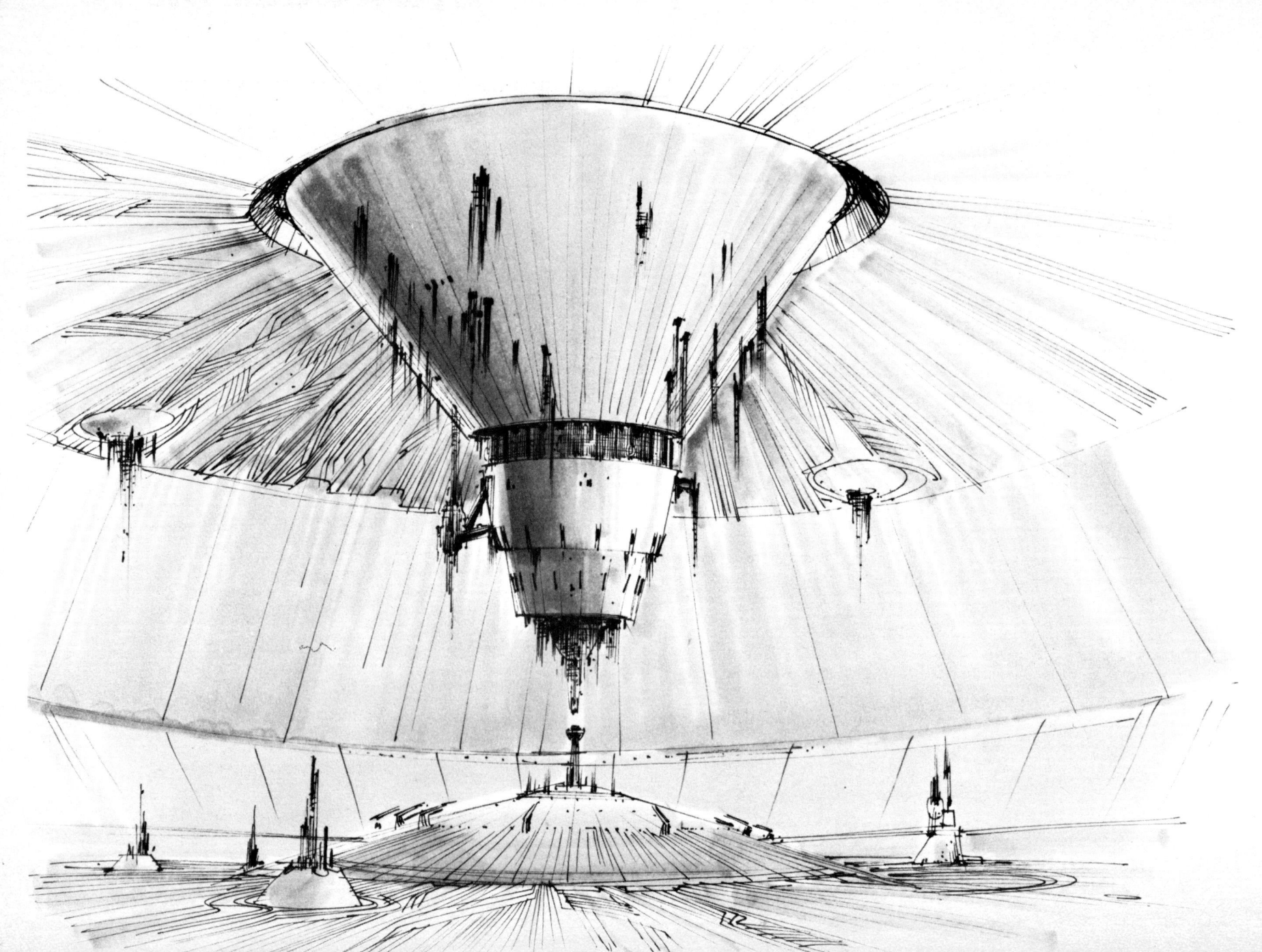

Introduction

Two and a half years before the release of RETURN OF THE JEDI, the artists whose work is included in this book began discussions with George Lucas about the design of the vehicles, settings and creatures that would appear in JEDI.

Joe Johnston, Art Director-Visual Effects, Nilo Rodis-Jamero, Assistant Art Director, and Ralph McQuarrie, Conceptual Artist, had each contributed to the designs used in THE EMPIRE STRIKES BACK. Johnston, as storyboard artist, and McQuarrie, as conceptual designer, had worked on STAR WARS as well.

After the initial meeting with Lucas, each artist worked on a particular concept—for example, the Imperial shuttle—then met again with him, where the designs were examined and discussed. Some were eliminated and others were approved for further development. In subsequent meetings during the next year, each vehicle or creature underwent further alteration and refinement as it evolved toward its final form.

Because of the collaborative method of working, not all of the designs included here show a linear development toward the final JEDI designs. There are variations on a theme, experiments that were dropped, as well as designs that, for practical reasons, were modified as the model makers and creature builders carried them to the next stage of development. Some of the captions running near the illustrations are comments and instructions for design alteration.

These drawings, then, represent the earliest visual representations of the hardware and inhabitants of RETURN OF THE JEDI. There is Jabba the Hutt's domain on Tatooine; the Death Star and its Imperial weaponry; Endor with its forest creatures; and the Rebel Alliance's newest technology.

Joe Johnston was raised in Texas, and studied art at Pasadena City College and industrial design at California State University at Long Beach. In 1975 he started work on STAR WARS as storyboard artist and designer, and was the Art Director-Visual Effects for both THE EMPIRE STRIKES BACK and RAIDERS OF THE LOST ARK. In addition to creating new vehicle and weapons concepts for JEDI, he was responsible for all of the storyboards involving special effects sequences.

Nilo Rodis-Jamero studied industrial design at San Jose State College, and worked as a designer of cars, boats, industrial vehicles, and military tanks before joining Lucasfilm in 1978. After beginning the preproduction designs for JEDI, he also designed the costumes with Aggie Rodgers, was involved with videomatics (video storyboards), and worked on the special effects storyboards. He was the Assistant Art Director for RAIDERS OF THE LOST ARK and Art Director for POLTERGEIST.

Ralph McQuarrie was born in Gary, Indiana, and studied illustration at Vancouver Technical School in Canada as well as at the Art Center College of Design in Los Angeles. Beginning in 1975, he created the earliest STAR WARS designs in a series of production paintings, and was the conceptual artist for both THE EMPIRE STRIKES BACK and RETURN OF THE JEDI. His other credits include CLOSE ENCOUNTERS OF THE THIRD KIND, BATTLESTAR GALACTICA, and conceptual paintings for E.T.

Norman Reynolds, Production Designer for RETURN OF THE JEDI, received an Oscar for his art direction on STAR WARS and was also production designer for THE EMPIRE STRIKES BACK. Born in London, he began working on films in 1962 and his most recent credits include BEHIND THE IRON MASK and SUPERMAN.

TATOOINE

| 10 | TATOOINE
Jabba the Hutt |

Jabba the Hutt

Jabba the Hutt was the first creature that the artists worked on. The starting point for the character was George Lucas's suggestion that Jabba have a sluglike body; the first image that occurred to Rodis-Jamero was that of a queen bee, a helpless creature who is catered to and cared for but who exerts an enormous amount of power within a small, enclosed world. Some of Ralph McQuarrie's early drawings of Jabba's face show him with sagging flesh and a head that droops down over his shoulders, completely obliterating his neck. Joe Johnston drew an early close-up of Jabba's face, similar to McQuarrie's sketches, but here the cunning of the character is more evident. Nilo Rodis-Jamero added a pair of stubby arms with almost useless hands, and eyes that were almond shaped and sinister looking. At this point, Phil Tippett, supervisor of stop-motion photography, took their drawings and built a model. In Tippett's sketch of his completed model (page 15) Jabba has several pairs of centipedelike legs. Tippett eliminated them in a second model, and Jabba the Hutt was complete.

TATOOINE
Jabba the Hutt | 11

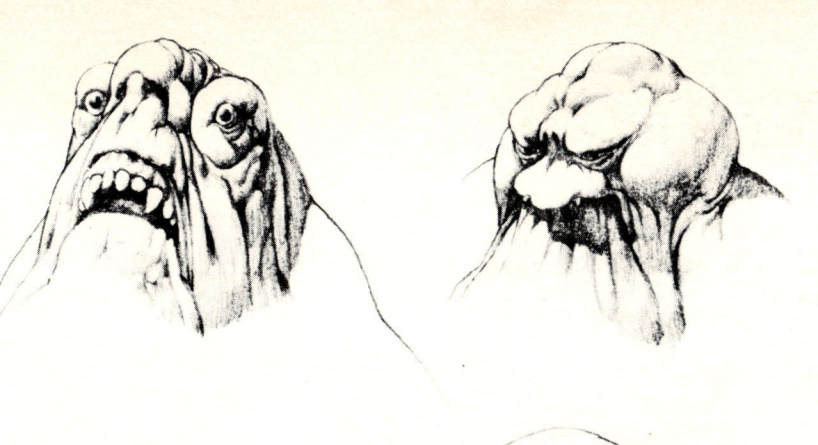

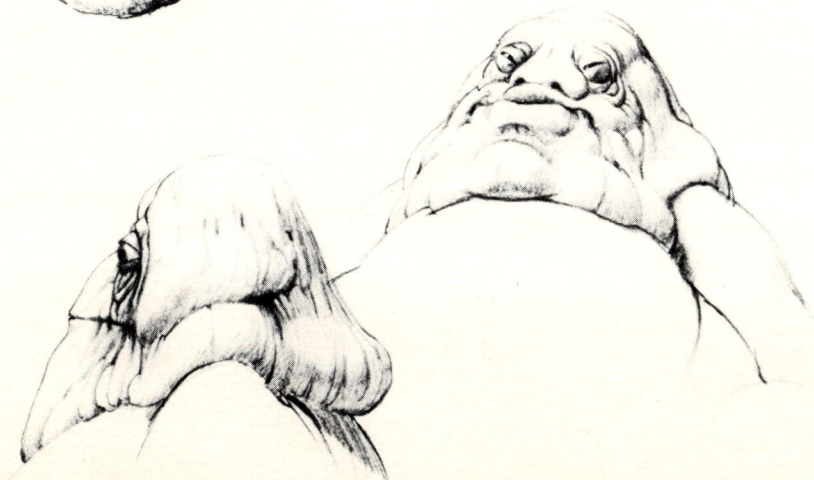

12 TATOOINE
Jabba the Hutt

TATOOINE
Jabba the Hutt
15

| 16 | TATOOINE Gamorrean Guards |

Gamorrean Guards

In Ralph McQuarrie's early sketches, Jabba the Hutt's palace guards were heavy, mean-looking creatures with gorillalike faces. Joe Johnston, however, began to draw the beasts as upright wild boars with horns and fangs. The guards were originally intended to be bare-chested and dressed in short gladiator-style costumes, but that proved impractical because it was too difficult to mold the creature's skin and still allow for shoulder movement. So the guards ended up wearing a cloth and leather uniform with protective metal epaulets that were decorative and also held the shoulder seams of the molded rubber body. It was Dave Carson in the Monster Shop who coined the name Pig guards, and this name is used interchangeably with the more formal name Gamorrean guards.

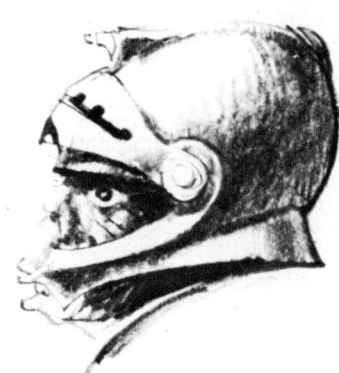

TATOOINE Gamorrean Guards 17

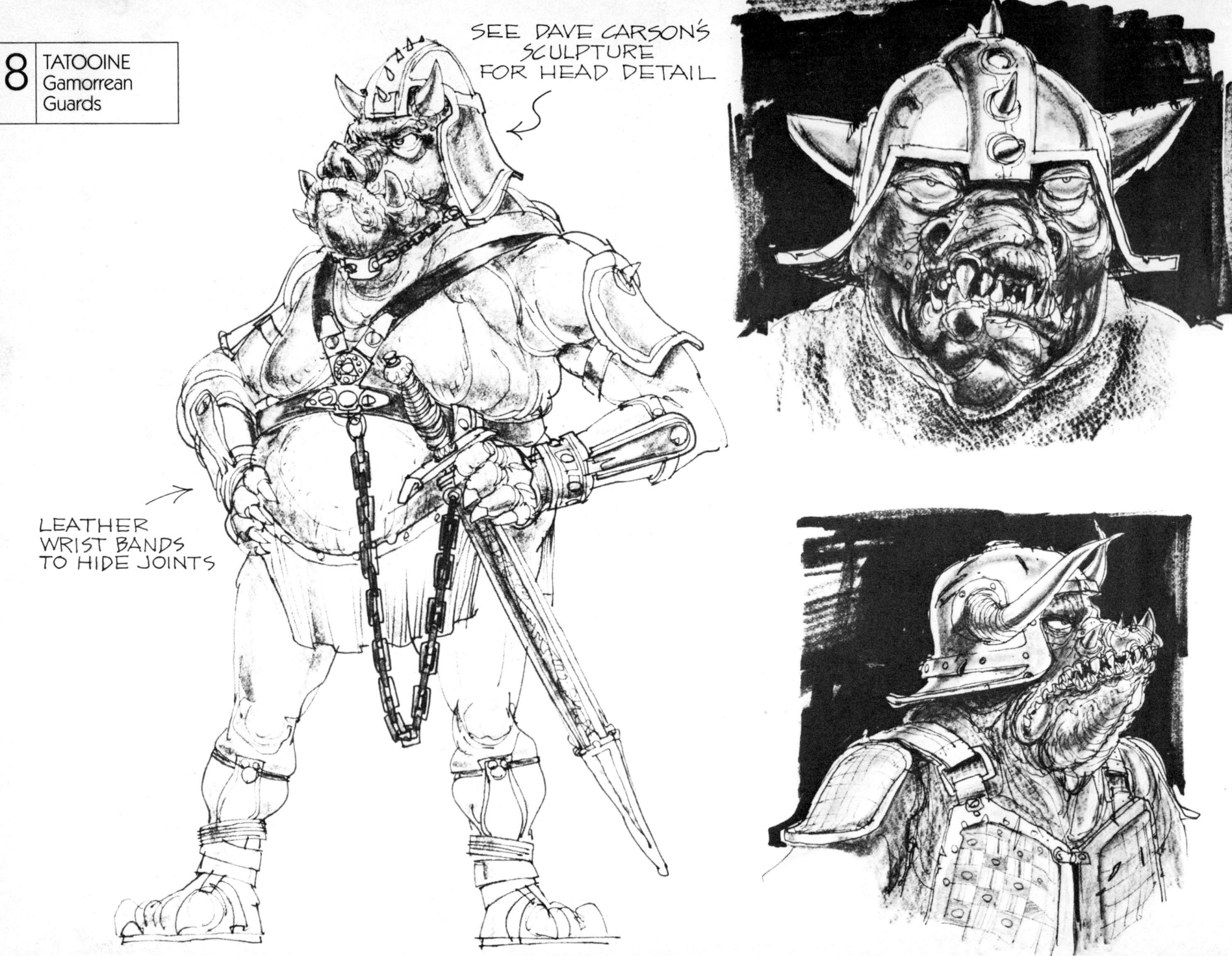

TATOOINE Gamorrean Guards 19

| 20 | TATOOINE Gamorrean Guards |

ASSORTED ALIENS — JABBA'S PARTY

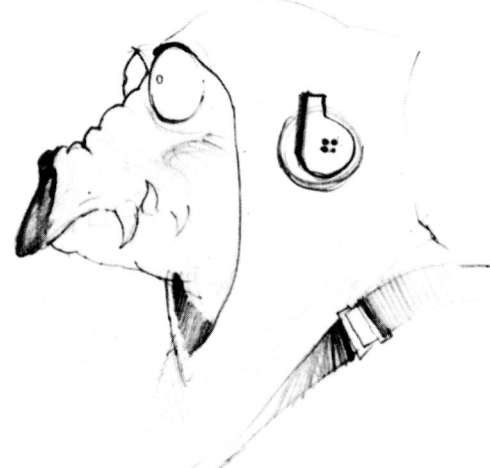

TATOOINE
Gamorrean Guards
21

22 TATOOINE — The Rancor

The Rancor

The first requirement for the monster was that it be able to grasp and lift objects with its front paws. The early sketches show it with massive, powerful shoulders, long arms, and extended fingers. Later it was decided that the Rancor would devour its victims, so it was given a set of powerful jaws and a large, fang-filled mouth. In an early stage (page 25) the Rancor was intended to be a man-in-a-suit and was given a semi-humanoid shape. Later the creature became a hand puppet, but this sketch was the jumping-off point for Phil Tippett's model design.

NOSE LOOKS LIKE EYES... DOWN PLAY NOSTRILS

ENLARGE HANDS

| 24 | TATOOINE
The Rancor |

GRASPING TUSKS

26 | TATOOINE
The Rancor

The Skiff and Jabba's Sail Barge

TATOOINE
Skiff and
Sail Barge
27

The earliest design of the antigravity desert skiff is a sort of pirate ship style, as seen in Joe Johnston's initial drawings. Originally, the skiff had sails because it was supposed to skim above the desert floor of Tatooine like Jabba's barge; but the skiff sails were dropped for practical reasons. It would be nearly impossible to recreate the sail and its movements with miniatures in the studio; in location filming, the sails would block both the action and the barge in the background. The skiff is designed as a service vehicle, with a flat bottom to reduce drag and increase speed; the controls are in the rear of the 30-foot-long boat, and it is operated by one helmsman.

Jabba's Sail Barge was designed by Ralph McQuarrie and underwent very little change from his earliest concept to the final form.

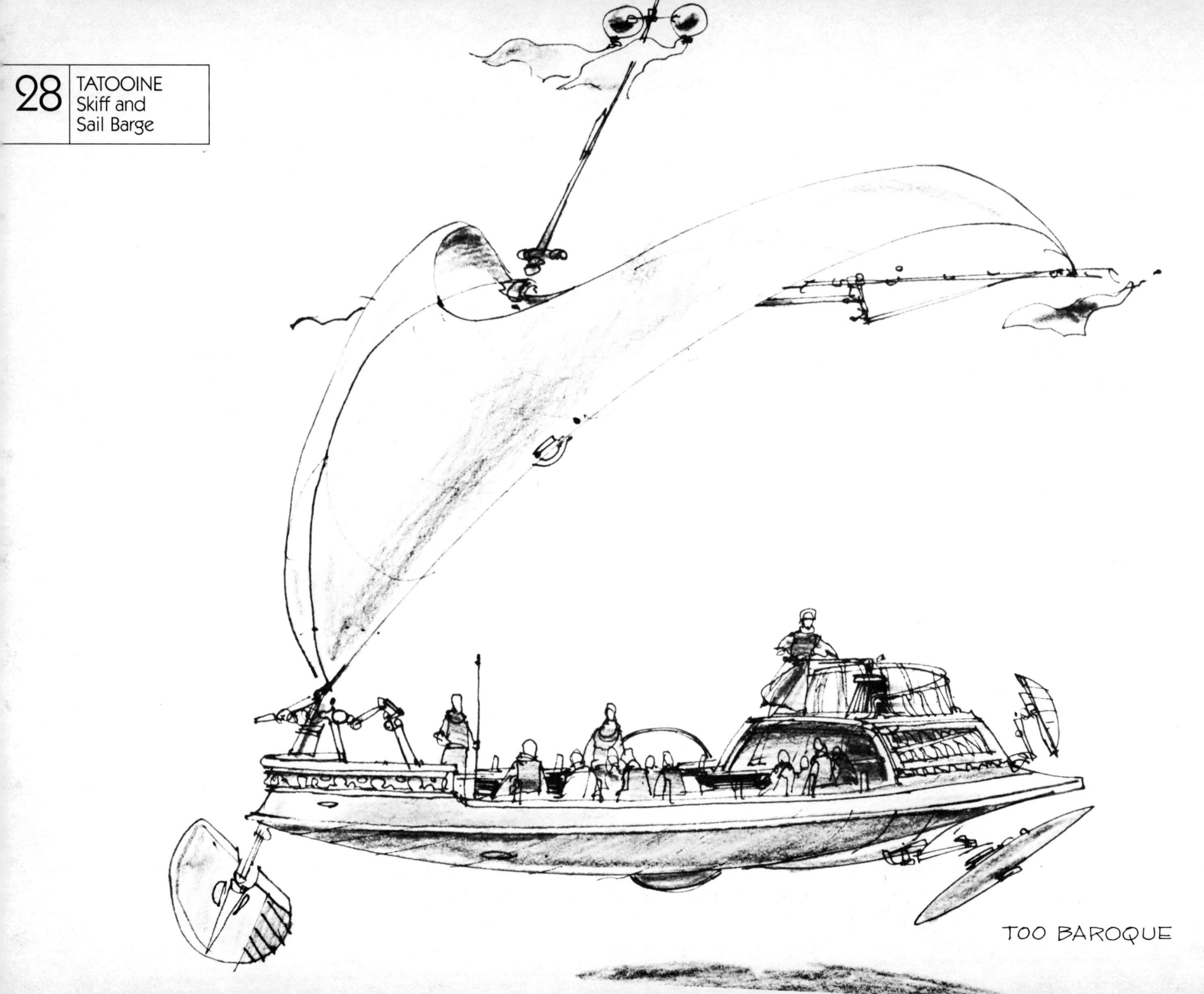

28 | TATOOINE Skiff and Sail Barge

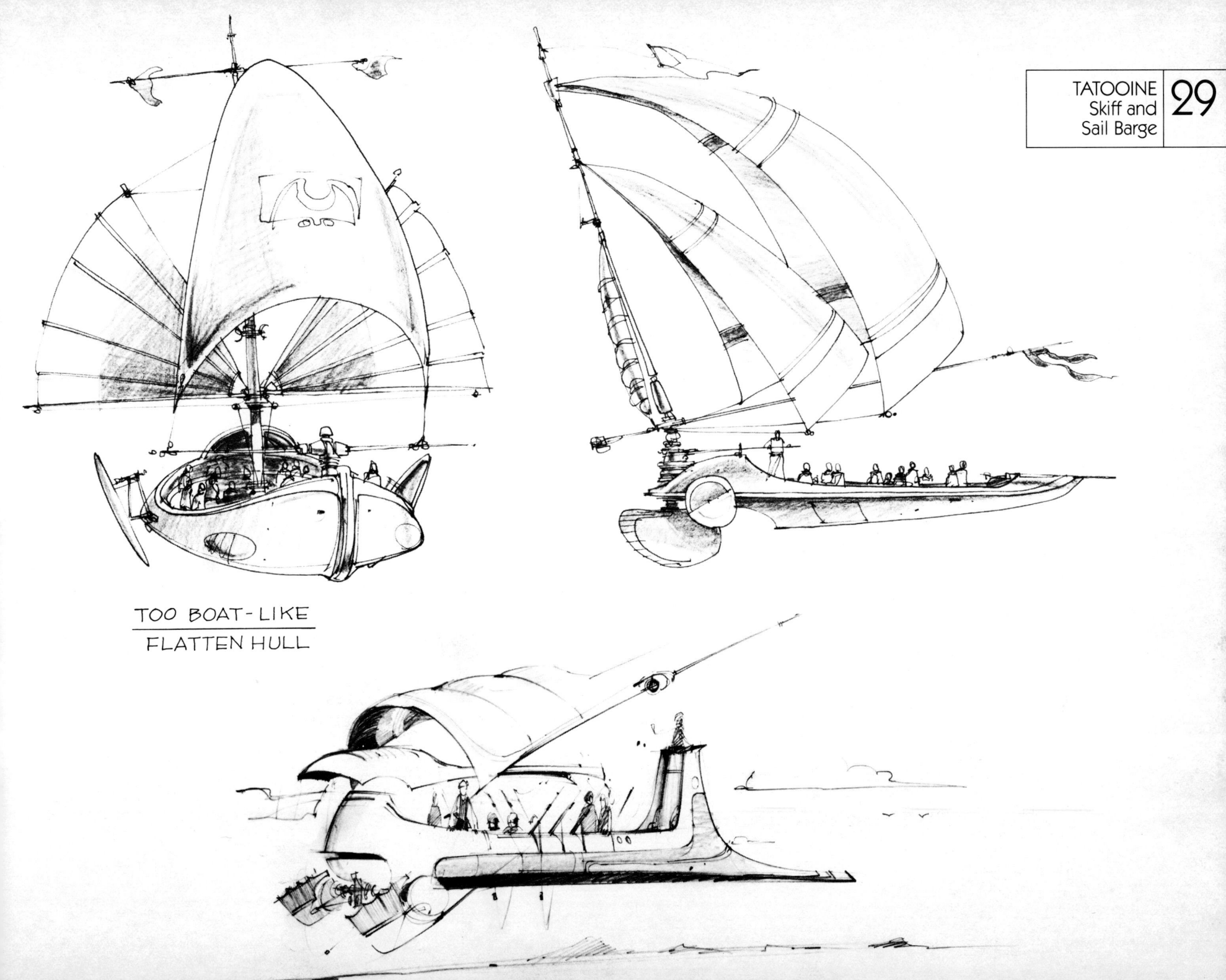

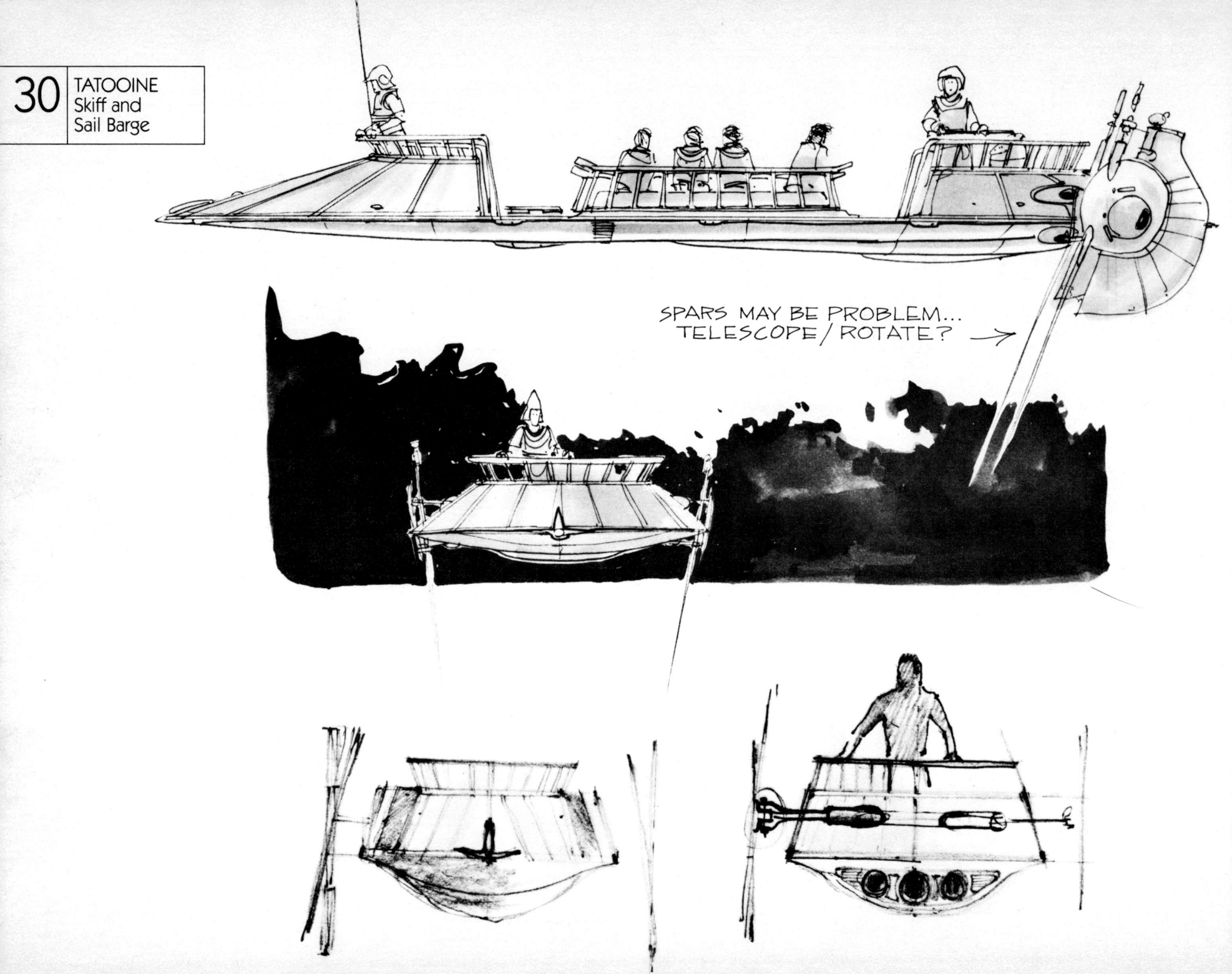

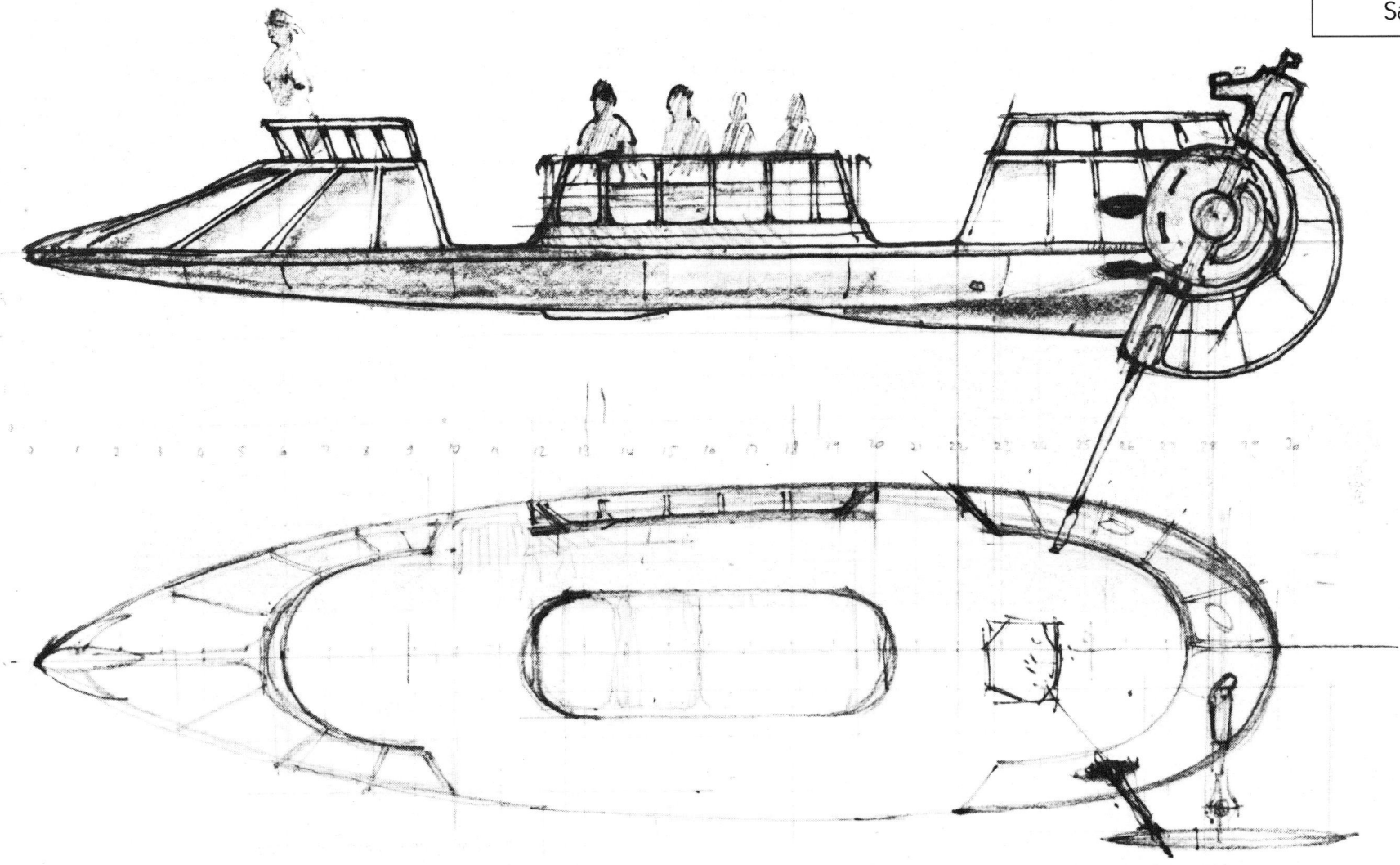

TATOOINE
Skiff and Sail Barge
31

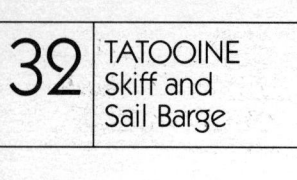

32 TATOOINE
Skiff and Sail Barge

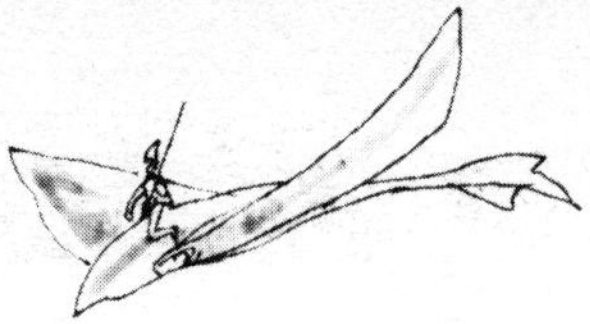

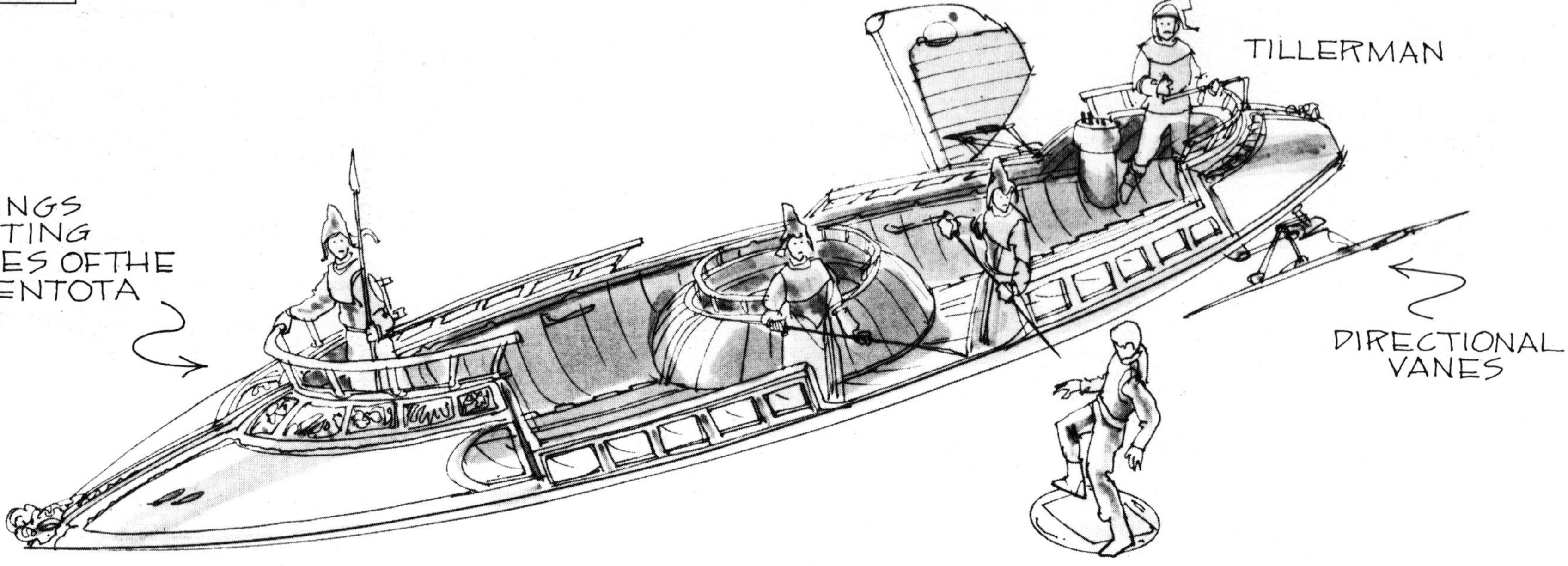

CARVINGS DEPICTING PHASES OF THE KO HENTOTA

TILLERMAN

DIRECTIONAL VANES

THE DISK OF FATE

TATOOINE
Skiff and Sail Barge
33

JABBA'S CUPOLA

| 34 | TATOOINE Skiff and Sail Barge |

ENDOR

36 ENDOR / Ewoks

Ewoks

The green Moon of Endor was originally going to be inhabited by two groups of creatures: the forest-dwelling Ewoks and the plains-dwelling Yuzzum. The Yuzzum had round, furry bodies supported by stiltlike legs, but they proved too difficult and costly to create in large numbers. Instead the Yuzzum became one of the creatures in the background of Jabba's court.

The Ewoks became more important. From the beginning it was decided that they would walk upright, and all the sketches show them standing on their hind feet. Some of Ralph McQuarrie's drawings depict them as stubby animals with large snouts; another early idea from Rodis-Jamero was to show them as tree critters: owllike mammals that sit in the branches of the Endorian trees and simply watch the action around them. Then the artists hit upon the more rotund, longer-haired concept for the Ewoks and developed the large, intelligent eyes and pug-nosed face. George Lucas liked this concept, so Joe Johnston did a series of drawings to establish exactly how the Ewok fur would look, how they would walk, and how they would hold weapons. Although they acquired more humanlike expressions and qualities, the Ewoks were always intended to be simple, primitive beings very much attuned to their forest environment.

THEY LOVE TO BOUNCE
UP AND DOWN

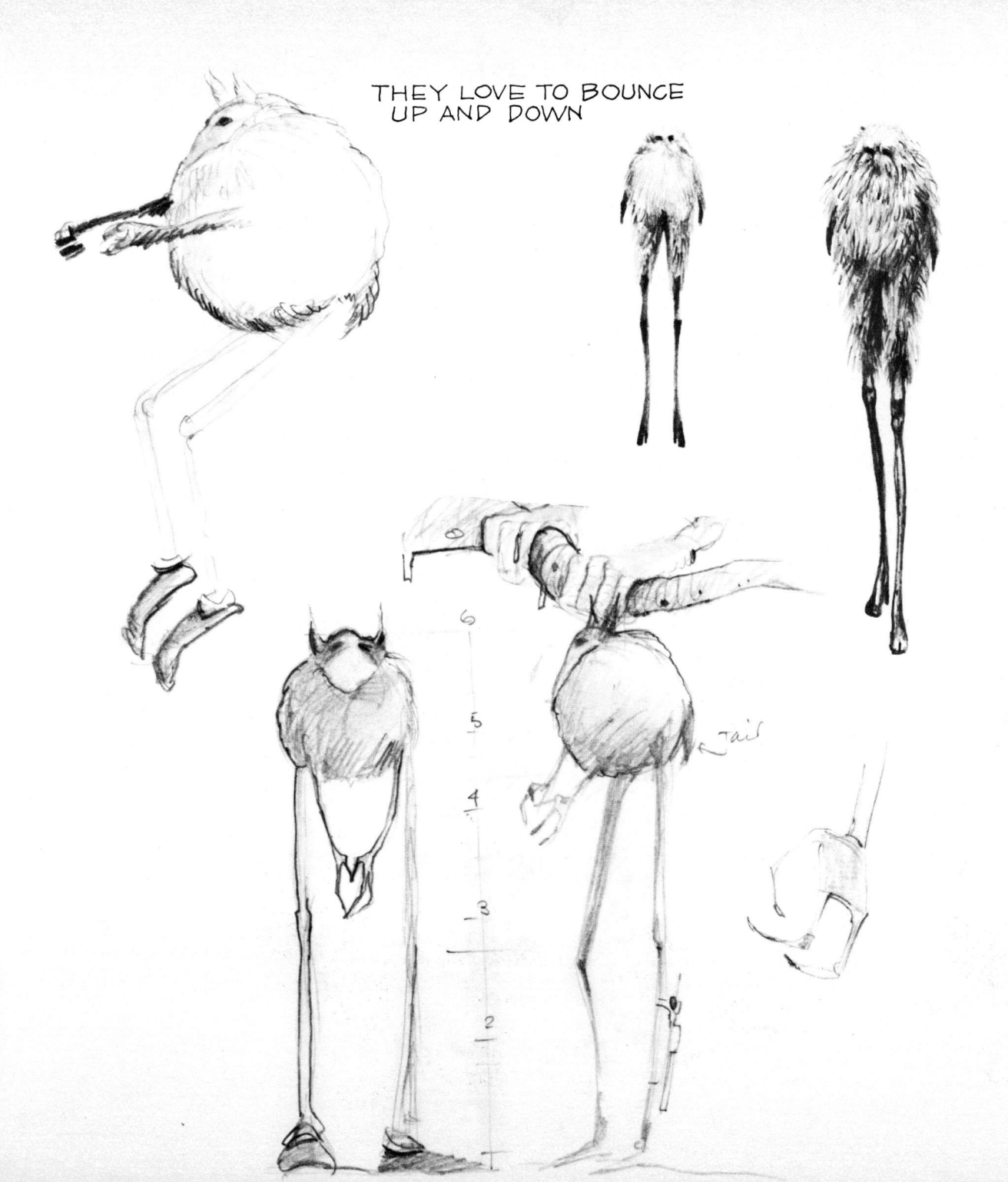

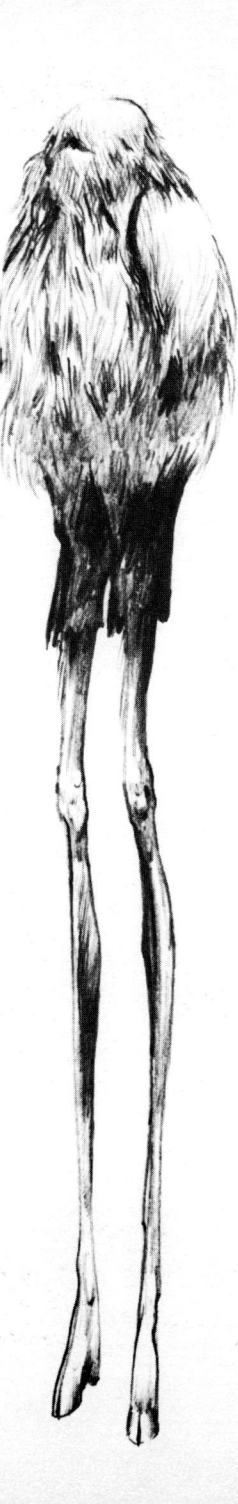

ENDOR
Ewoks 37

| 38 | ENDOR Ewoks |

EWOKS BASKING IN THE SUN ON A TREE BRANCH

ENDOR
Ewoks | 39

HUMAN-LIKE PROPORTION

40 | ENDOR Ewoks

SLING SHOT

MORE EWOKS

ENDOR
Ewoks   41

42 | ENDOR
Ewoks

ENDOR
Ewoks | 43

HOODS TO HELP HIDE
NECK SEAM

44 ENDOR Flying Ewoks

Flying Ewoks

The original idea for Ewok air transportation was to have them ride primitive-looking birds, but the birds would have been technically difficult and expensive to film so the decision was made to keep the Ewoks' flying machines very simple. Hang gliders were introduced, and they fit perfectly with the simple Ewok weapons and primitive forest culture.

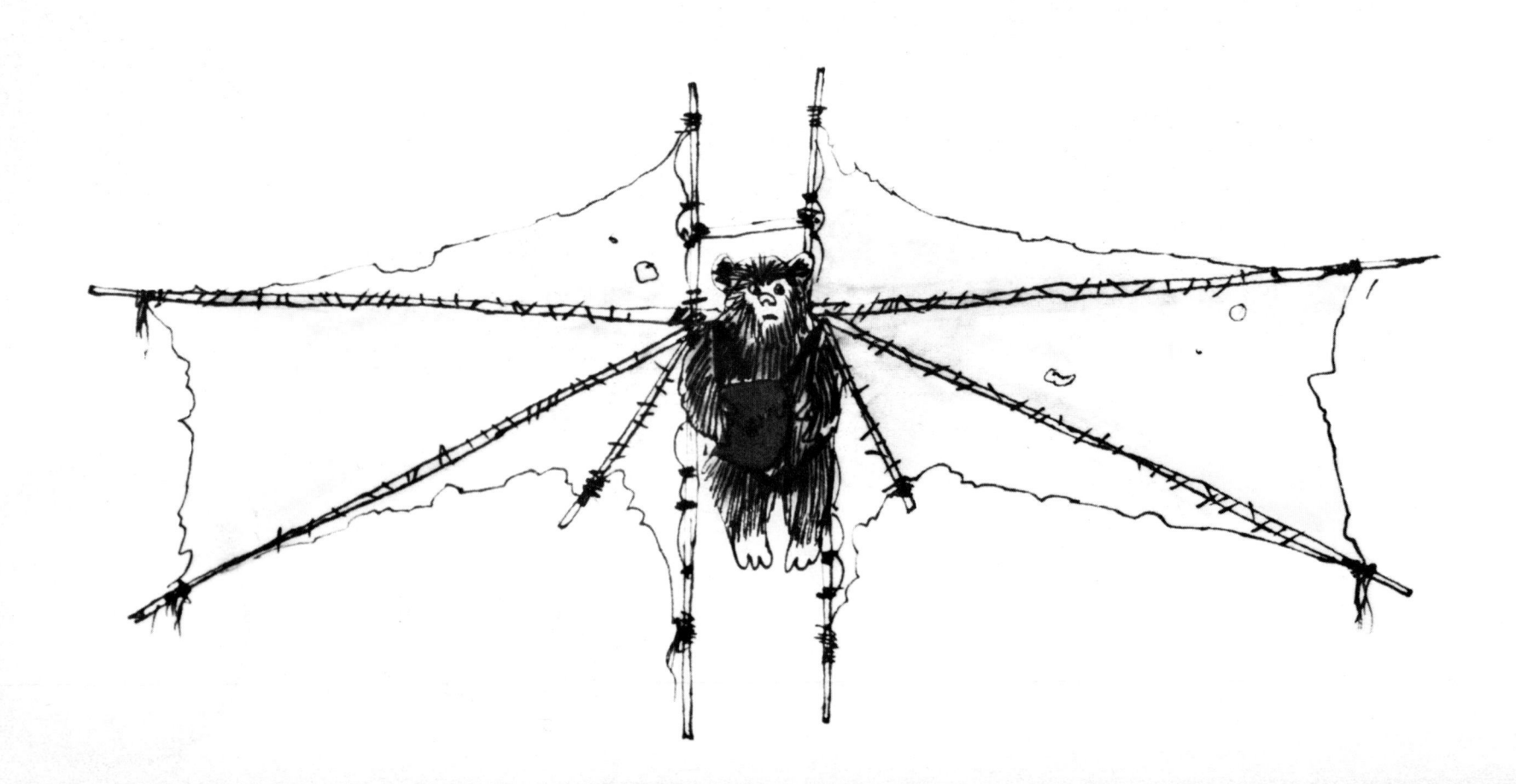

ENDOR
Flying Ewoks 45

SAVE FOR
PROJECT "X"

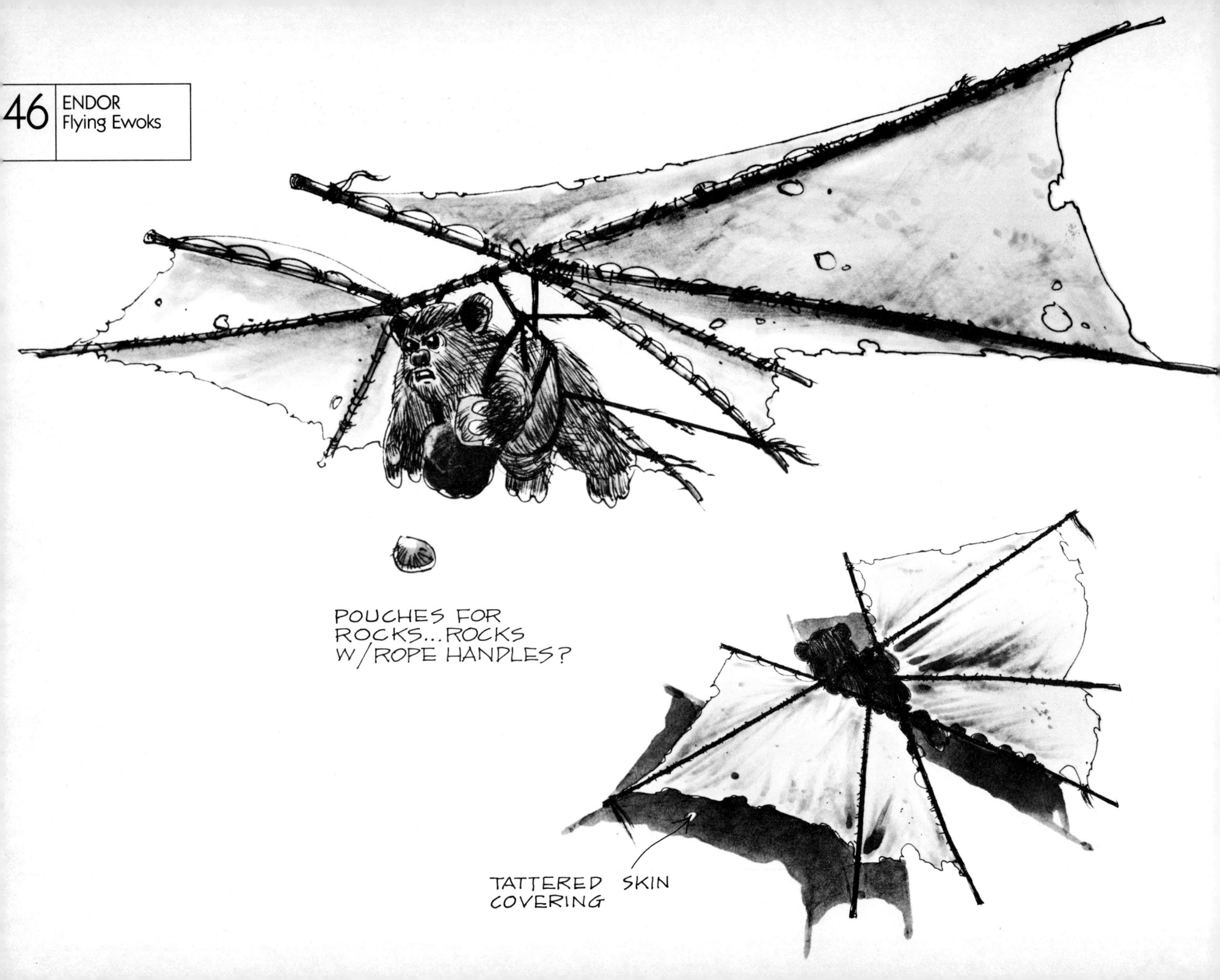

46 ENDOR
Flying Ewoks

POUCHES FOR ROCKS... ROCKS W/ ROPE HANDLES?

TATTERED SKIN COVERING

Speeder Bikes

ENDOR
Speeder Bikes
47

George Lucas's first request was for a rocket-powered "scooter"; some of Rodis-Jamero's early drawings show the speeder bikes as blocky and square-shaped with a large engine in the rear and controls in the foot pedals. In an early McQuarrie sketch the bikes were sleek with spaceshiplike fins and a large, clear windshield, but with no real sense of a power source. When the artists let their imaginations roam, the bikes took on the characteristics of souped-up hot rod cars and heavy-duty motorcycles with large, complicated engines (page 50). The big breakthrough in the design came with the forked front end; in later sketches the bikes became smaller and the engine, still in the rear, also became smaller while the entire design acquired a slimmed-down look. Finally, Joe Johnston decided to try a three-dimensional approach and built a model of the bike, which was approved and became the final vehicle seen in the movie.

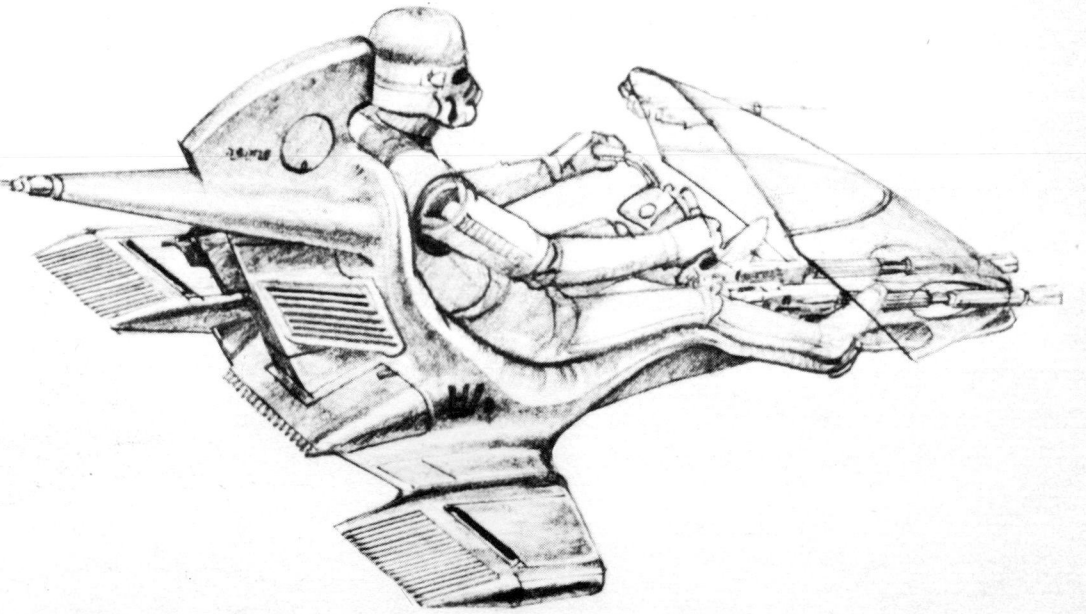

48 | ENDOR Speeder Bikes

ENDOR Speeder Bikes | 49

IMPERIAL SCOOTERS

| 50 | ENDOR Speeder Bikes |

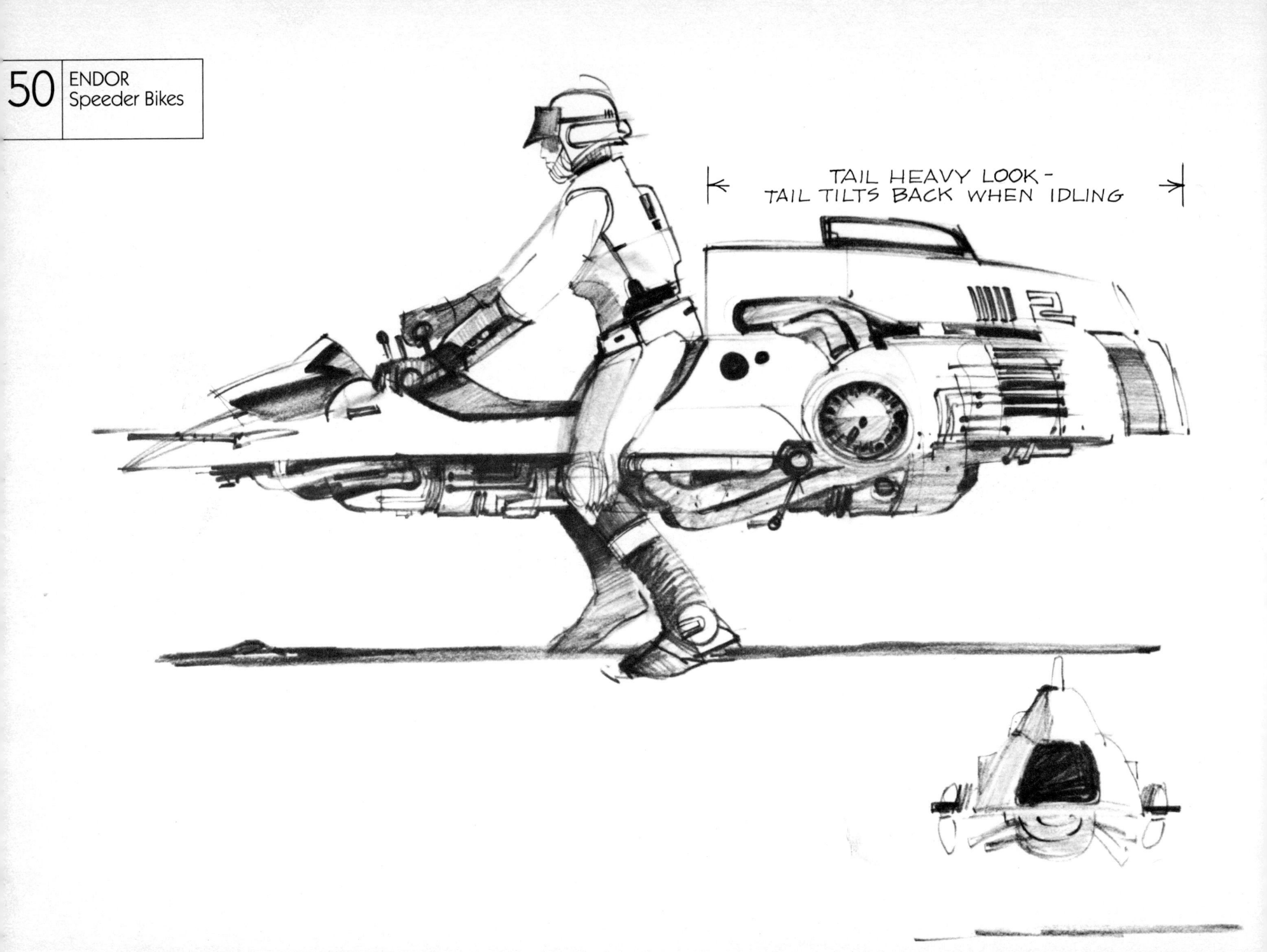

TAIL HEAVY LOOK —
TAIL TILTS BACK WHEN IDLING

ENDOR Speeder Bikes | 51

ALL-ENCLOSED MOTOR--
VERY LITTLE GREEBLIES
UNDERNEATH

| 52 | ENDOR Speeder Bikes |

MOVEABLE DIRECTIONAL VANES

FRONT HANDLE BAR ADJUST

ENDOR Speeder Bikes | 53

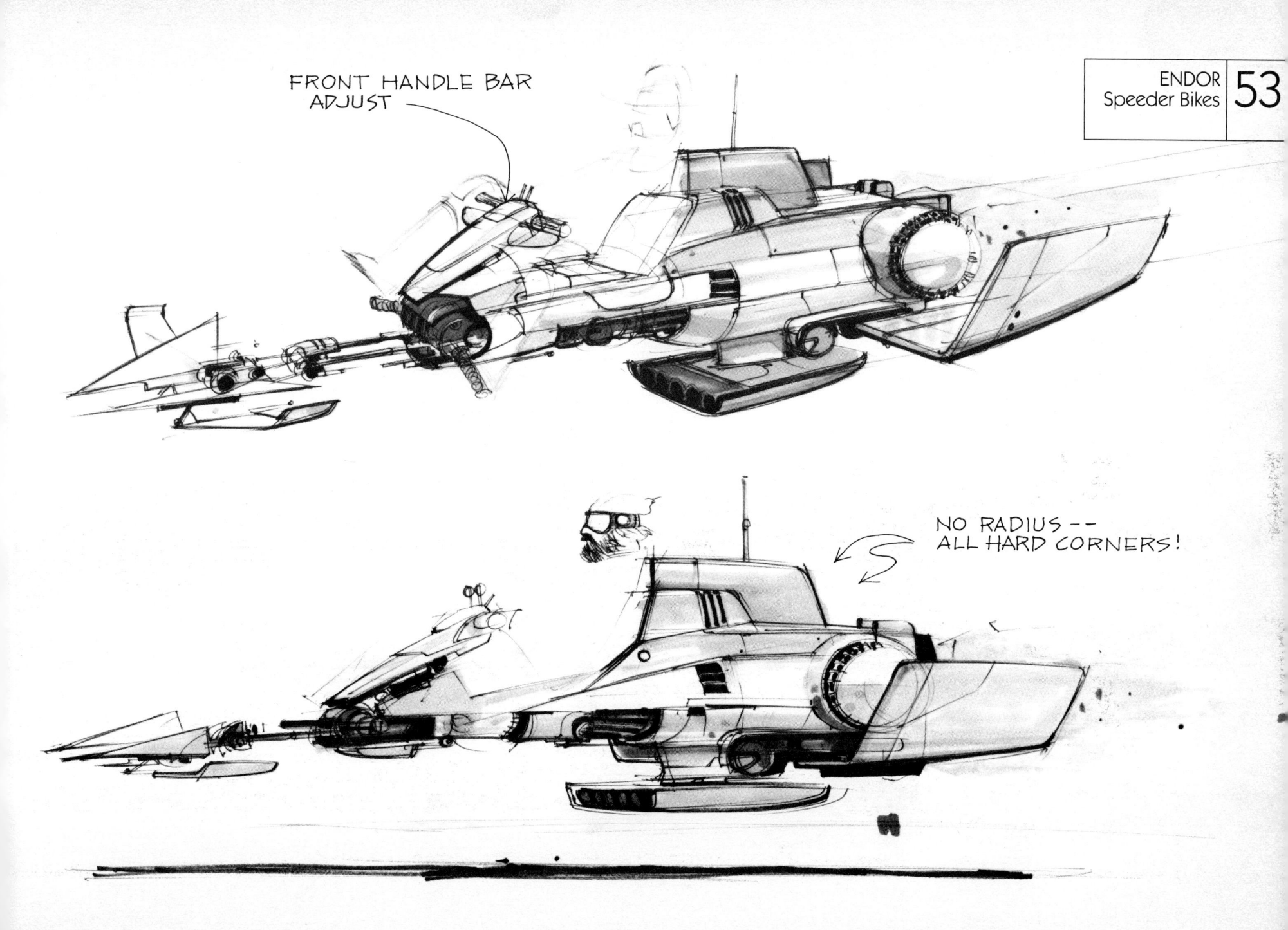

NO RADIUS -- ALL HARD CORNERS!

| 54 | ENDOR Speeder Bikes |

ENGINE WITH A SEAT

ENDOR Speeder Bikes | 55

| 56 | ENDOR
Speeder Bikes |

BIKES SHOULD BE WHITE OR
BRIGHTLY PAINTED, NOT
CAMOUFLAGED.

| ENDOR Speeder Bikes | 57 |

| 58 | ENDOR Speeder Bikes |

$2,795.00 (KIT FORM)

ENDOR
Speeder Bikes 59

60 | ENDOR Speeder Bikes

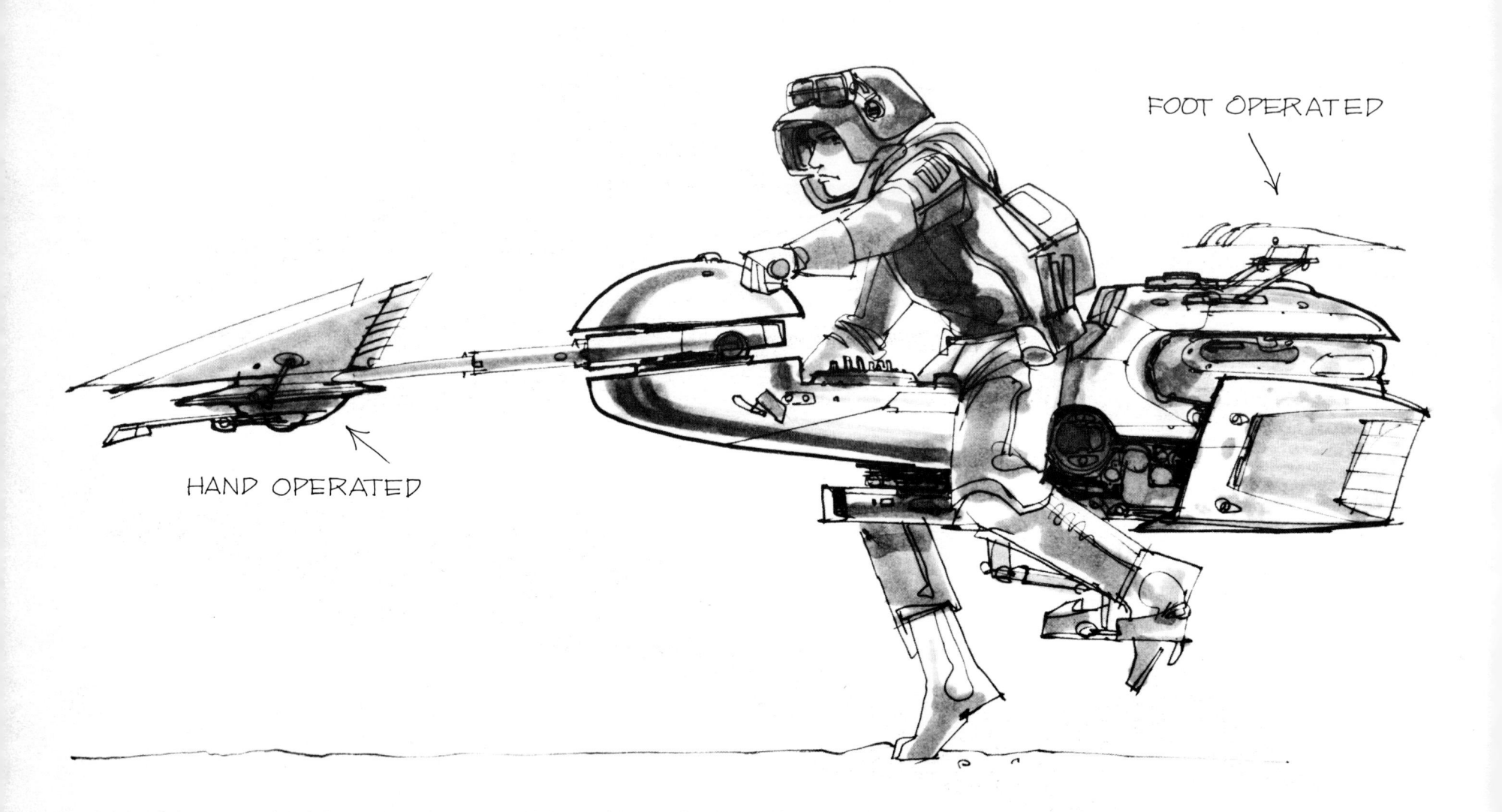

FOOT OPERATED

HAND OPERATED

ENDOR Speeder Bikes | 61

BIKES CAN HAVE
MISSING PANELS,
HOT ROD MODIFICATIONS,
ETC.

62 | ENDOR Imperial Scouts | *Imperial Scouts*

The uniforms for the Imperial biker scouts on Endor are similar to stormtrooper uniforms but they are simpler and more pared down, with pieces of white body armor attached to a black undergarment. There is a breastplate with connecting shoulder, elbow, and forearm pieces, and a wide, utilitarian belt. The helmets, with a built-in breathing apparatus and opaque eye covering, enclose and protect the entire head.

ENDOR Imperial Scouts 63

FOR SCALE REFERENCE ONLY.

SEE RONZANI FOR FINAL DETAILS.

MOUTH AREA TO BE ONE PIECE INJECTION

64 | ENDOR
Imperial Scouts

DELETE GUN

BREAST PLATE ENDS HERE. SEE MICK FOR DETAILS

SOFT SHELL CANVAS-- MUST FOLD

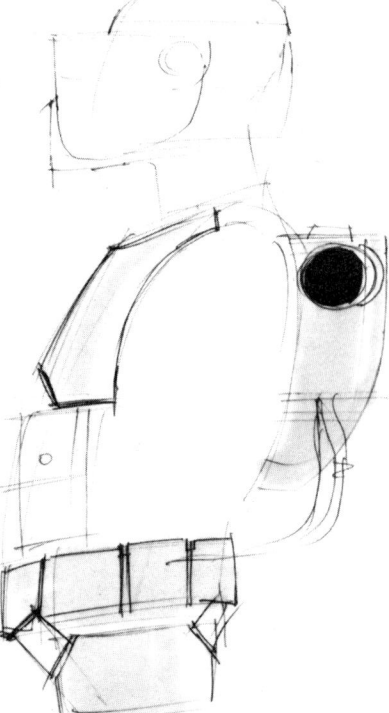

SEE IRA FOR DETAILS

THE DEATH STAR

66 DEATH STAR Unfinished Exterior

The Death Star
Unfinished Exterior

George Lucas's directive for the new Death Star was that it had to *look* unfinished on the outside. Therefore the drawings show the exterior surface as being incomplete on a large section of the sphere, making it possible to see the superstructure underneath. Even though the Death Star is operable, and capable of awesome destructive powers, Lucas felt that a finished exterior would present too formidable a foe to the Rebel forces. Unfinished, the Death Star appears much more vulnerable than it really is, and it is this illusion of vulnerability that lures the Rebels into planning an attack upon it.

DEATH STAR Unfinished Exterior | 67

SHOW LARGER CUTAWAY AREAS

| 68 | DEATH STAR
Unfinished
Exterior |

BREAK UP
UNFINISHED
EDGE
MORE

|—————————— 100 MI. ——————————|

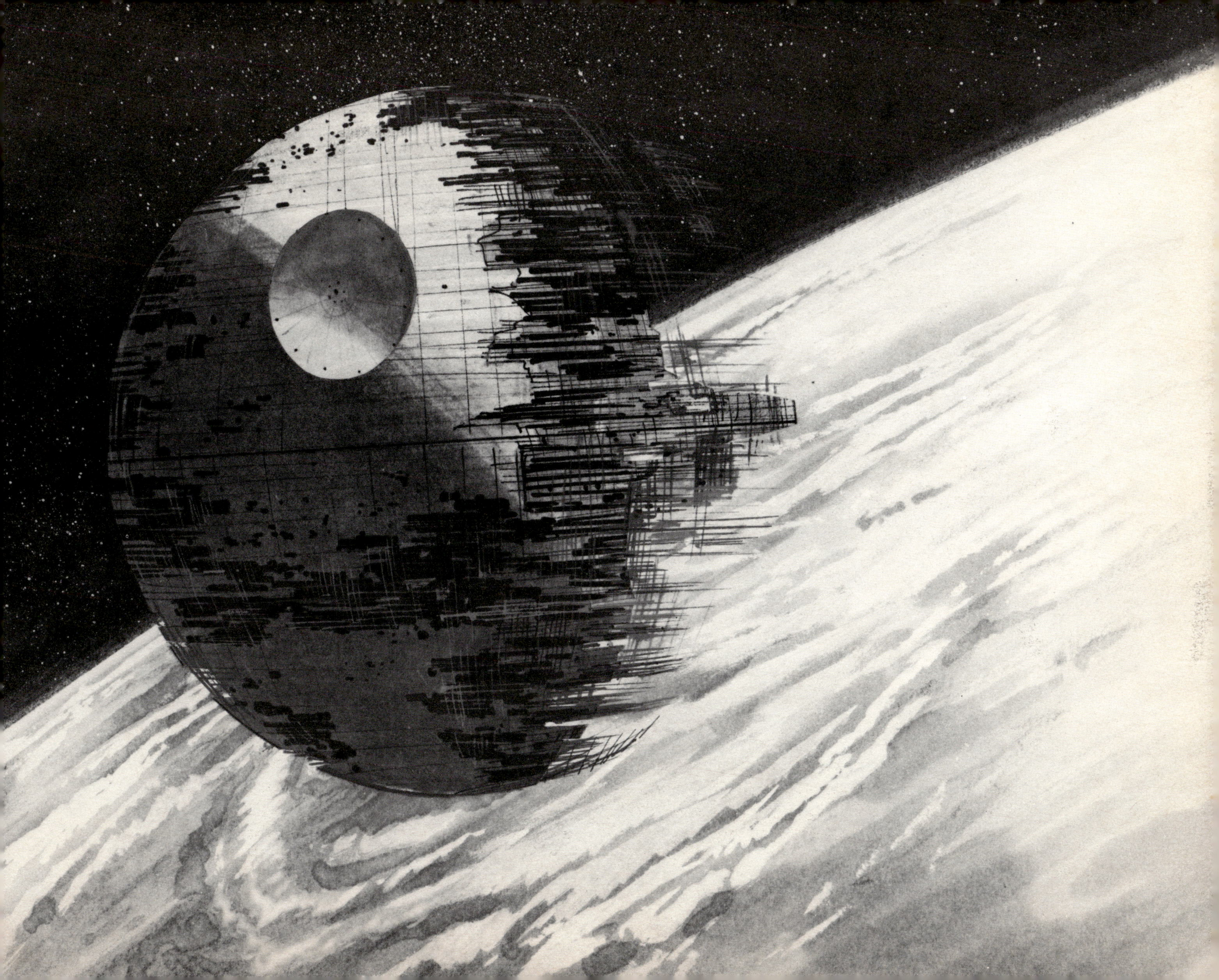

70 DEATH STAR Unfinished Exterior

LARGE SIZE DOCKING BAY (EMPEROR'S BAY)

The Shuttle

DEATH STAR
The Shuttle | 71

In early designs, the Imperial shuttle is shown with a square, boxlike body standing on multiple legs; another version has an airplane-inspired look and a large, round cockpit; and yet another is a bargelike plane with heavy front landing gear. The final design, however, came from two sources: a quick sketch of a TIE fighter pod with three wings, and the Skyhopper vehicle that was originally designed for STAR WARS, in which Luke Skywalker is seen playing with a Skyhopper model airplane. An important intermediate drawing in the development of the shuttle (page 73) shows a plane with three wings, the stationary top wing already in place and the round cockpit reflecting the earlier designs. Another early drawing by Norman Reynolds shows the shuttle with four upright wings, rather than three, connected to a central core (see below). The final ship is compact and streamlined, with folding wings and a sleek cockpit that opens from the bottom. Even though three shuttles are used in the movie—Darth Vader's, the Emperor's, and the Rebels' stolen *Shuttle Tydirium*—only one plane was built full size for the production.

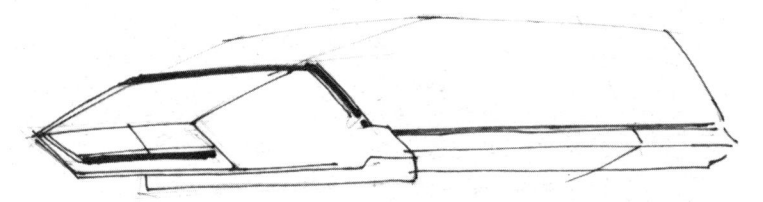

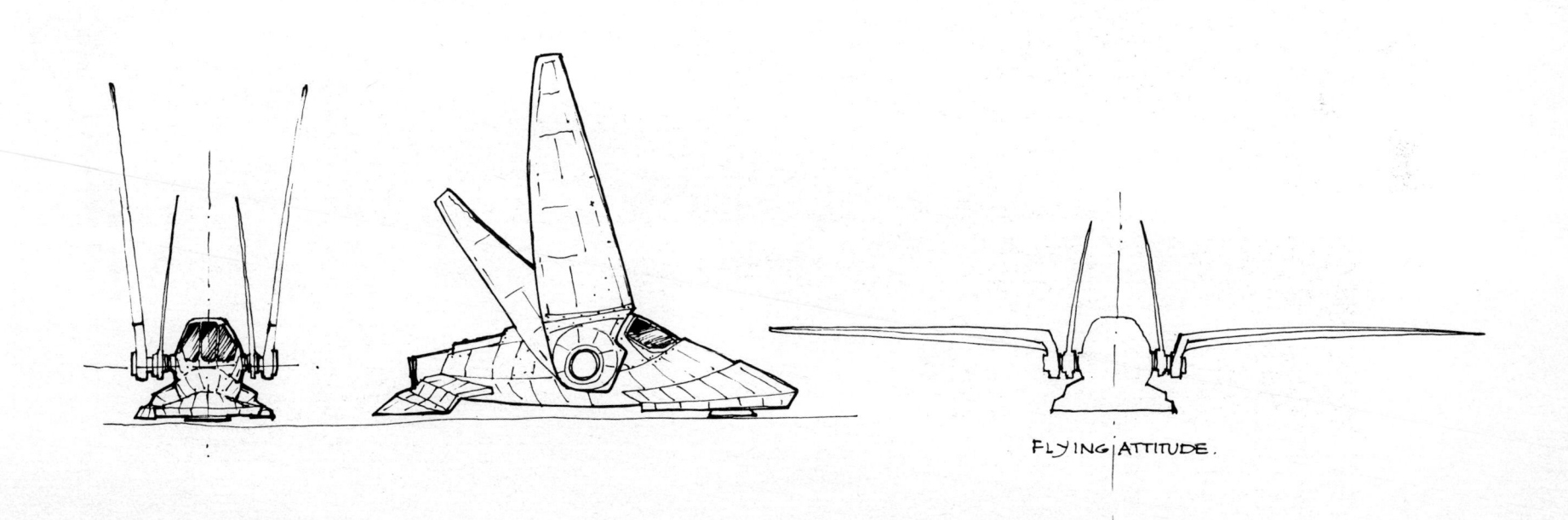

FLYING ATTITUDE.

72 | DEATH STAR
The Shuttle

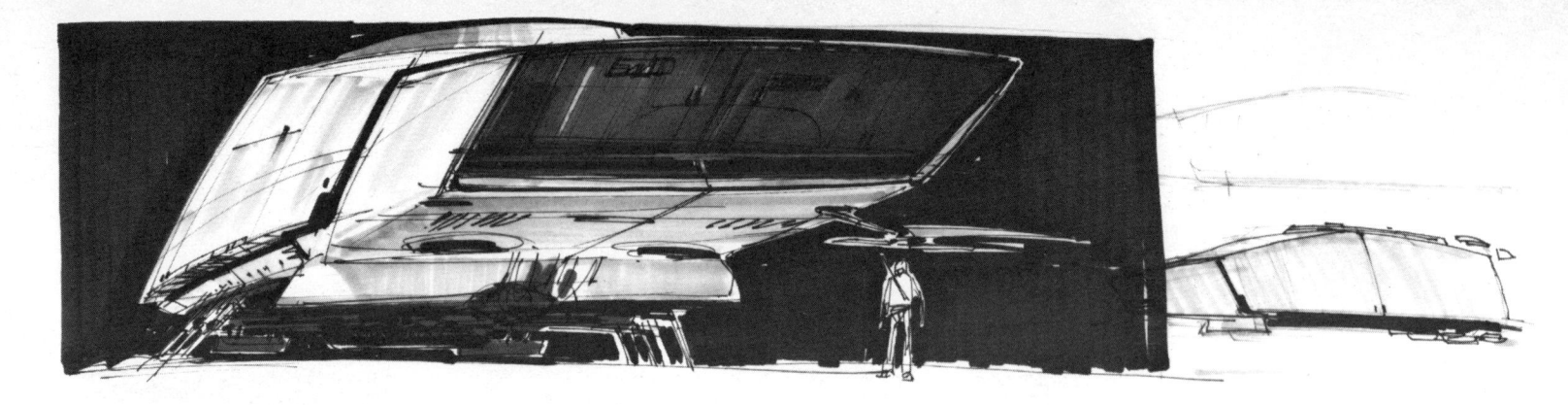

DEATH STAR
The Shuttle | 73

T.I.E. COMPONENTS

LANDING POSITION

74 | DEATH STAR
The Shuttle

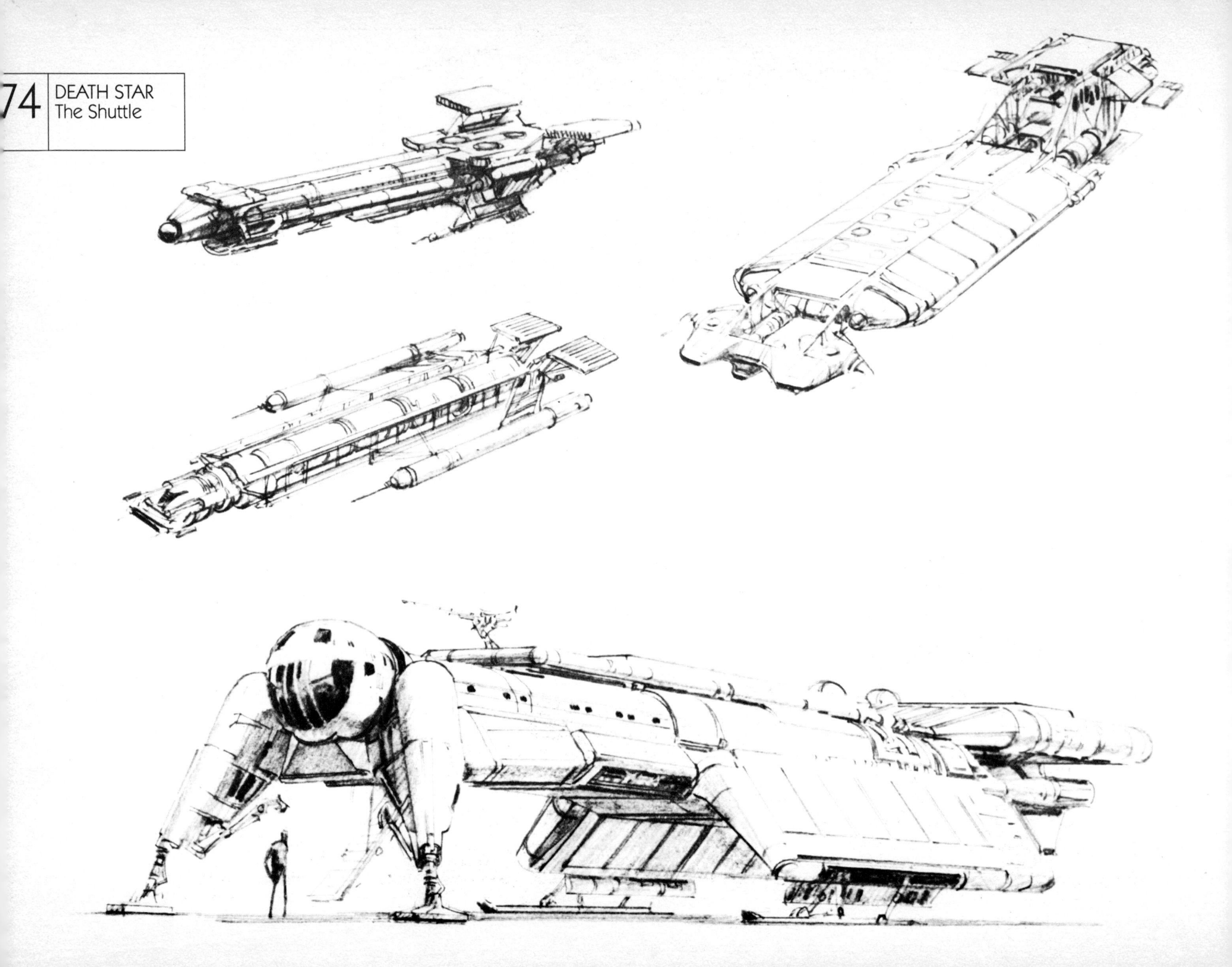

DEATH STAR
The Shuttle | 75

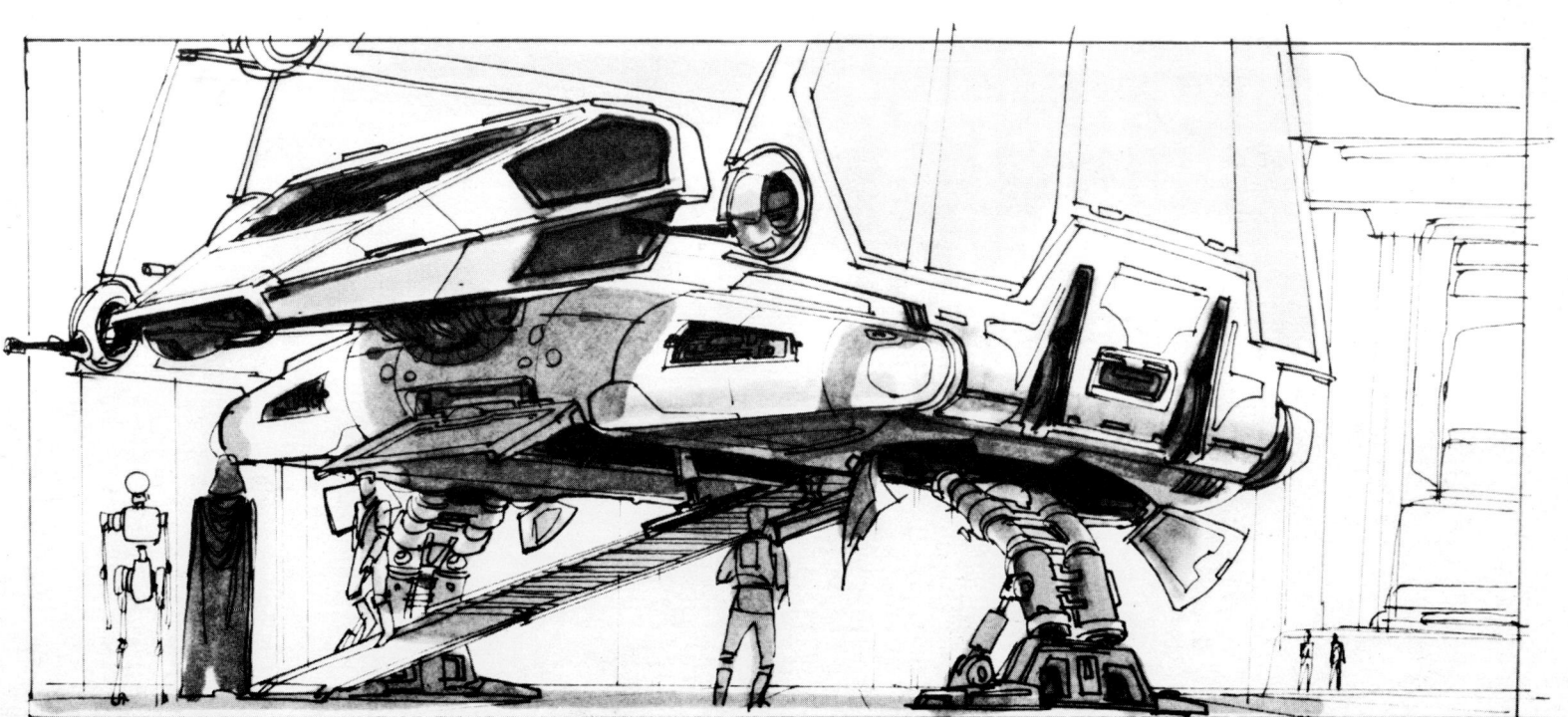

SKETCH FOR RAMP POSITION

DEATH STAR
The Throne Room
Interior, Death Star

The Emperor's throne went through several transformations before the final design of a large, contoured chair with control panels in the arms was reached. One early drawing (next page) shows the chair suspended from the ceiling, although in the final design it is base-mounted. Above the Emperor's throne, at this stage, there was a circular control mechanism that was replaced in the movie by a set of periscopelike devices. An early scheme for the throne room had the Emperor isolated on a platform with a treaded catwalk approach, and two swooping circular catwalks that connect the throne room to other parts of the Death Star (page 84). In the final design, the Emperor's throne stands at the head of a flight of stairs, with the elevator from the main docking bay across from it. Behind the Emperor's throne is a circular window with radiating spokes, a fitting background for the supreme ruler of the galaxy.

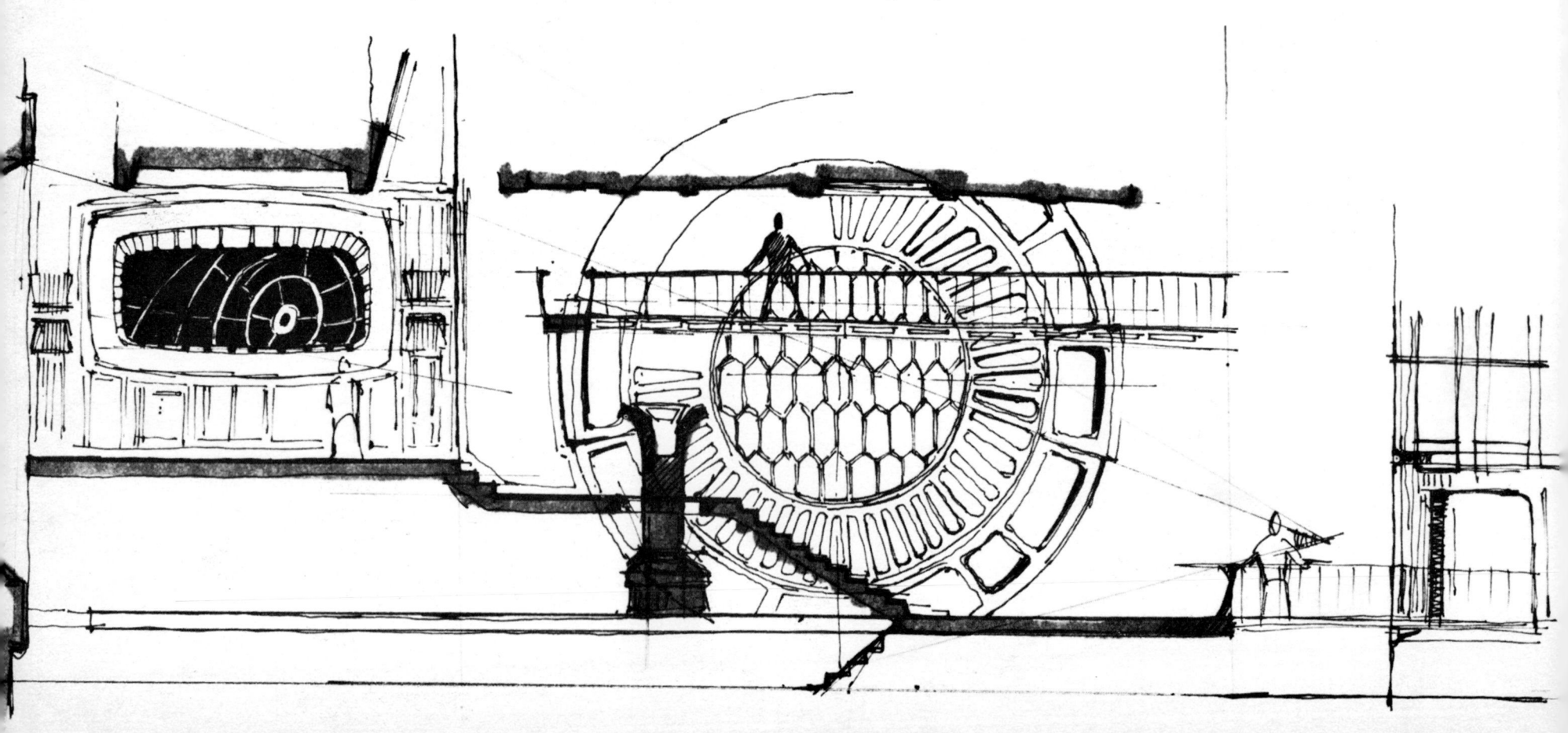

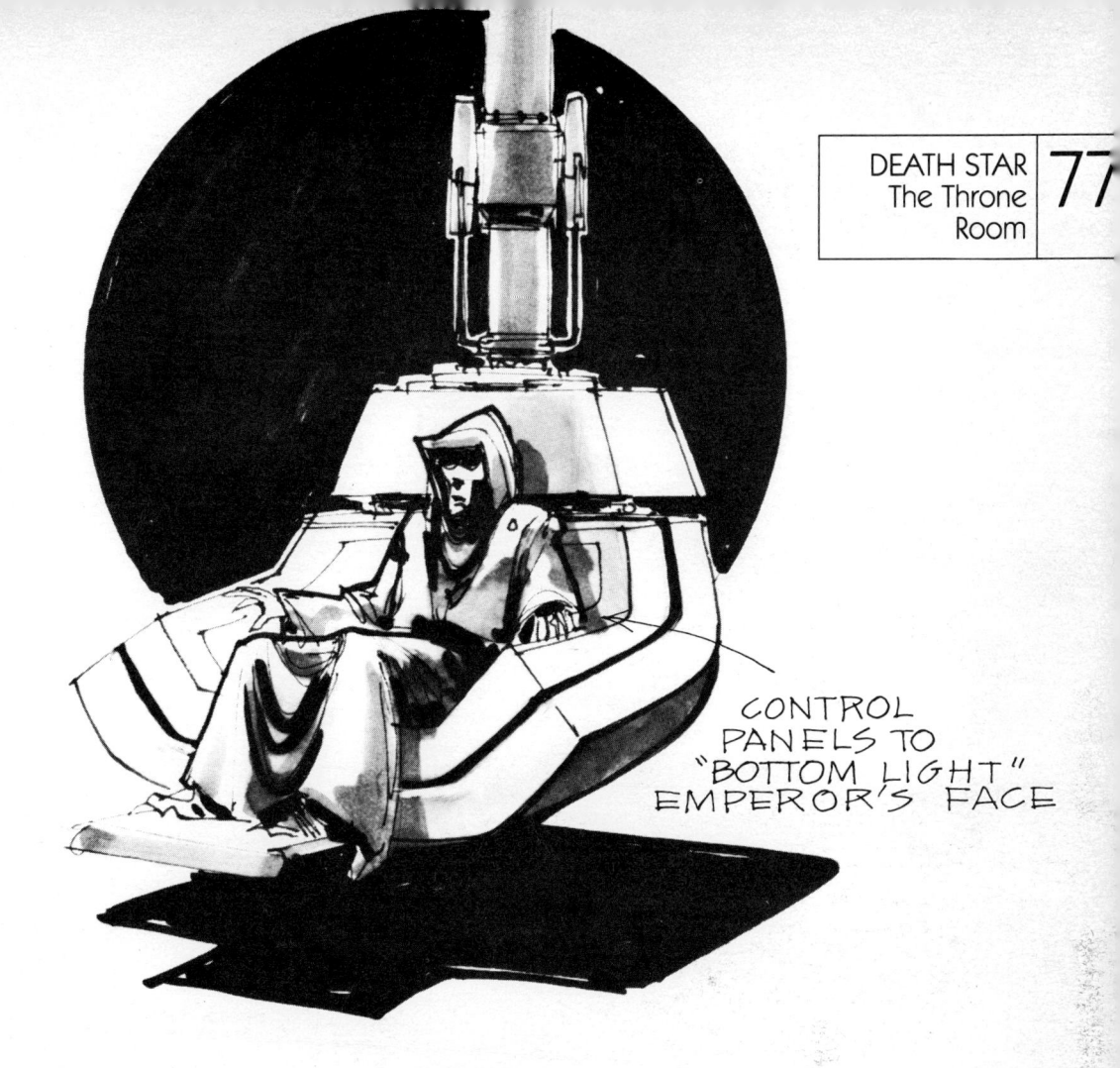

DEATH STAR
The Throne Room | 77

CONTROL PANELS TO "BOTTOM LIGHT" EMPEROR'S FACE

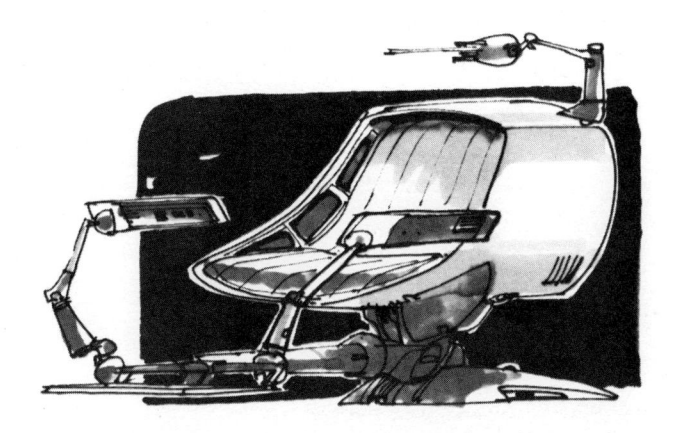

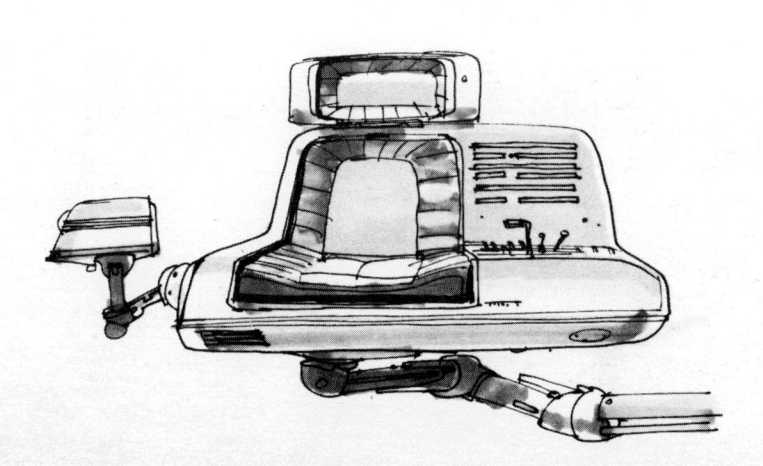

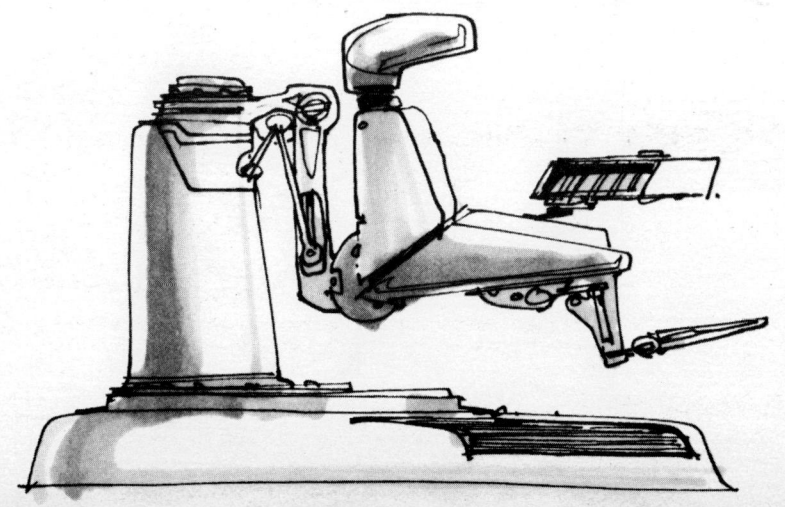

78 | DEATH STAR
The Throne Room

TWO SIDE SCREENS FOR READOUTS... WINDOW IN CENTER

CONTROL PODS

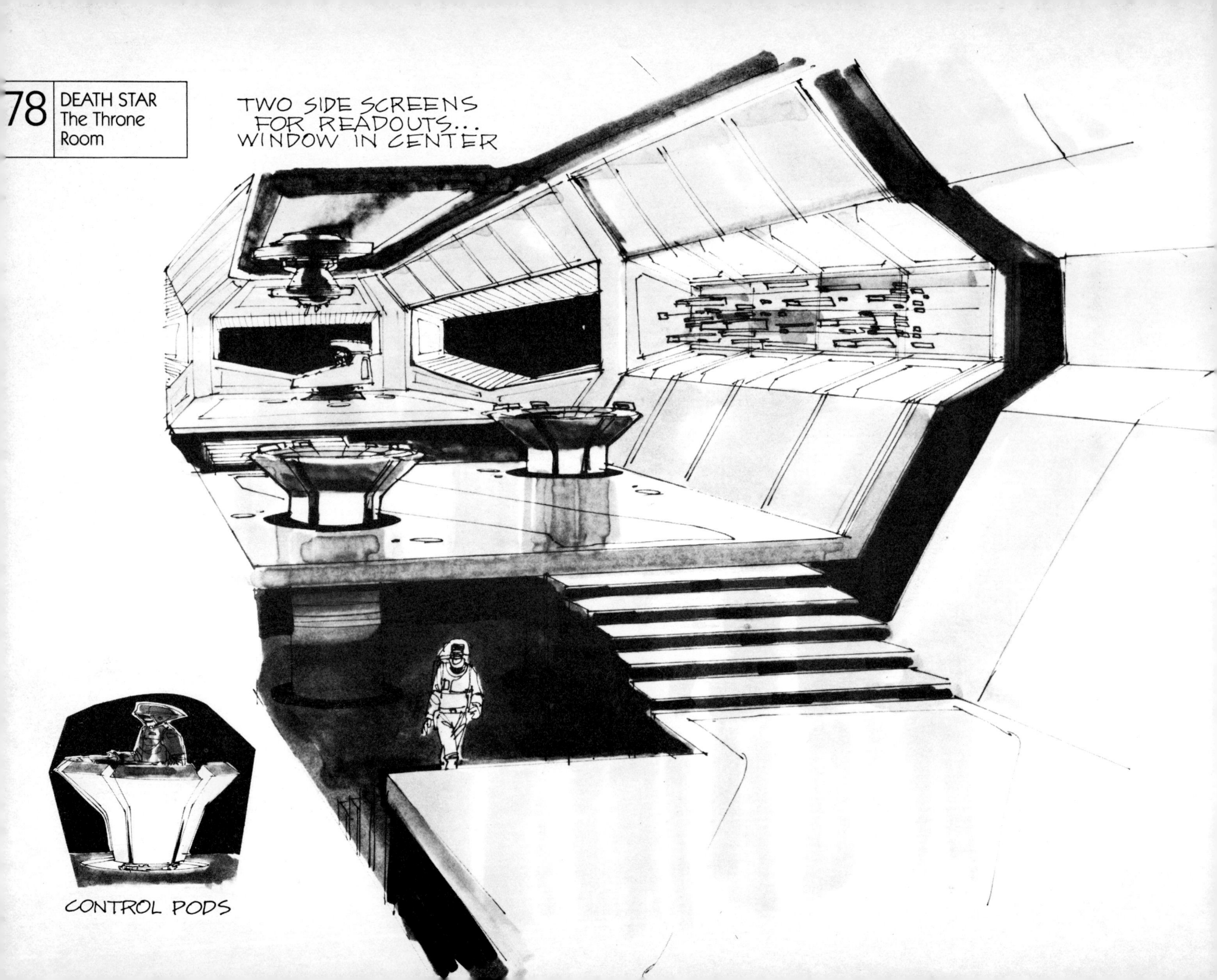

DEATH STAR | 79
The Throne Room

80 | DEATH STAR — The Throne Room

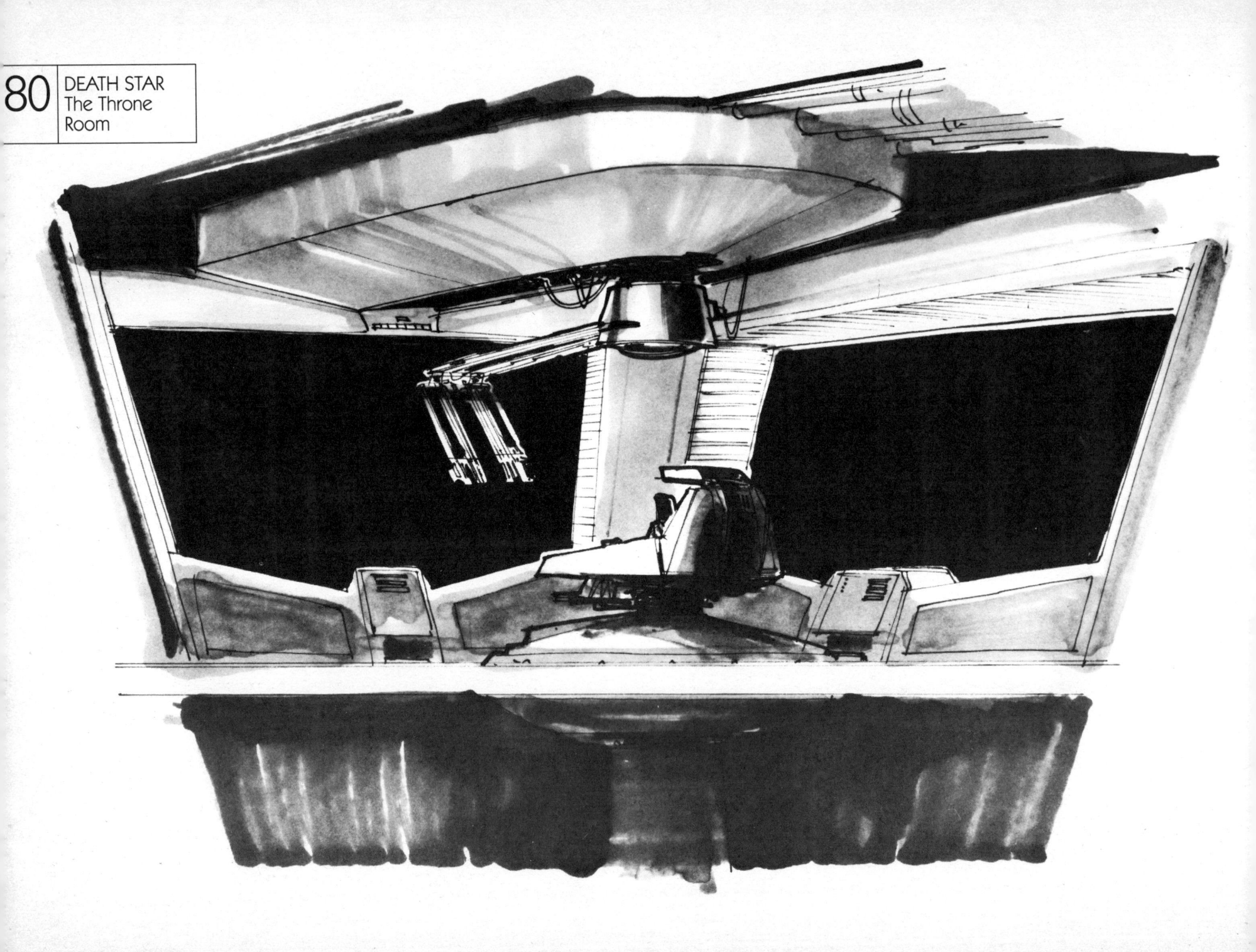

DEATH STAR | **81**
The Throne Room

NO SOLID FLOOR. CATWALKS AND PLATFORMS SUSPENDED OVER ABYSS.

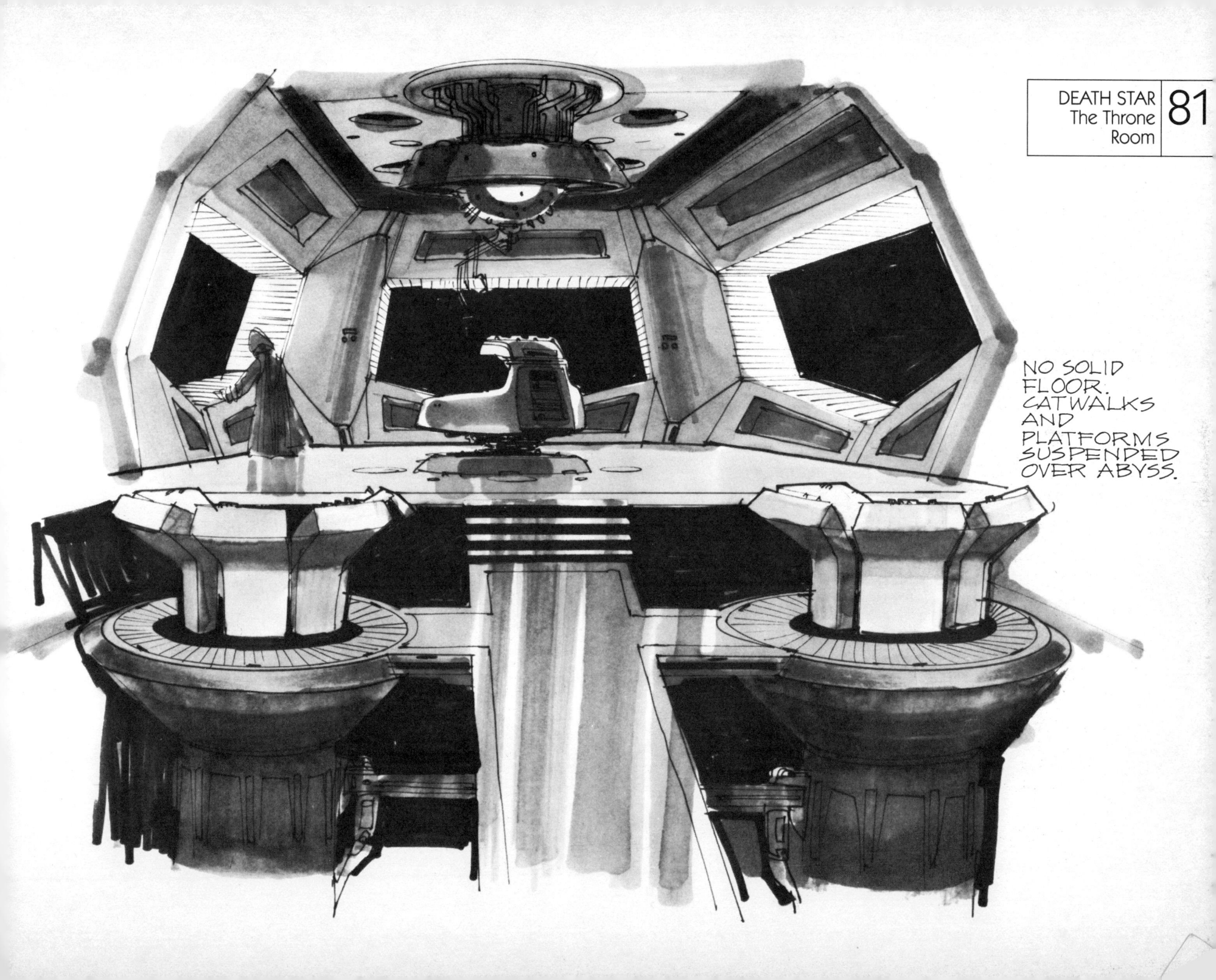

82 | DEATH STAR
The Throne Room

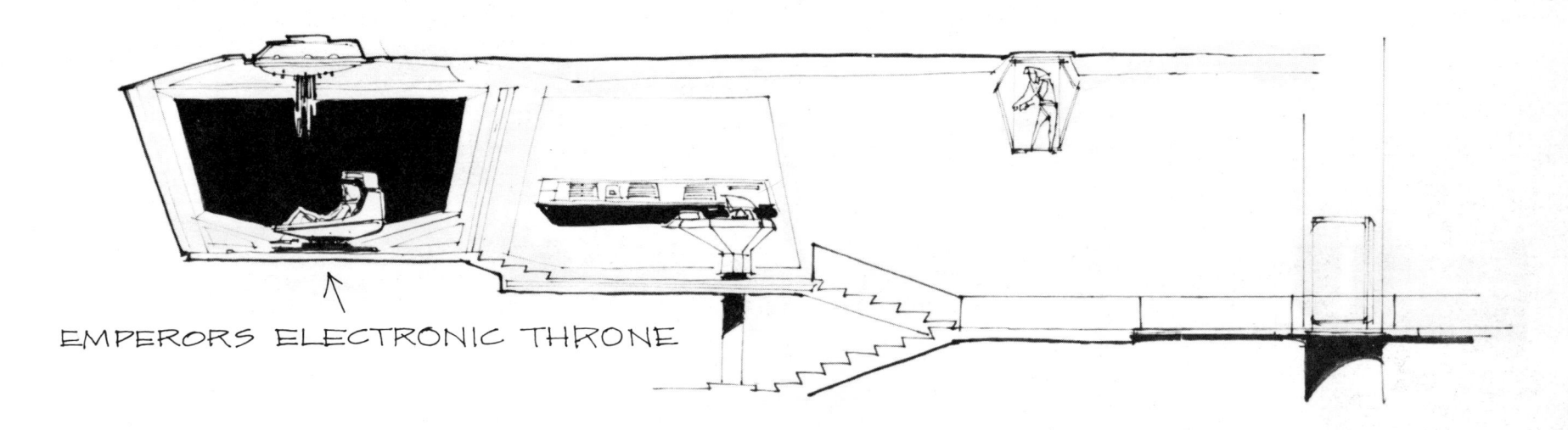

DEATH STAR
The Throne Room
83

EMPERORS ELECTRONIC THRONE

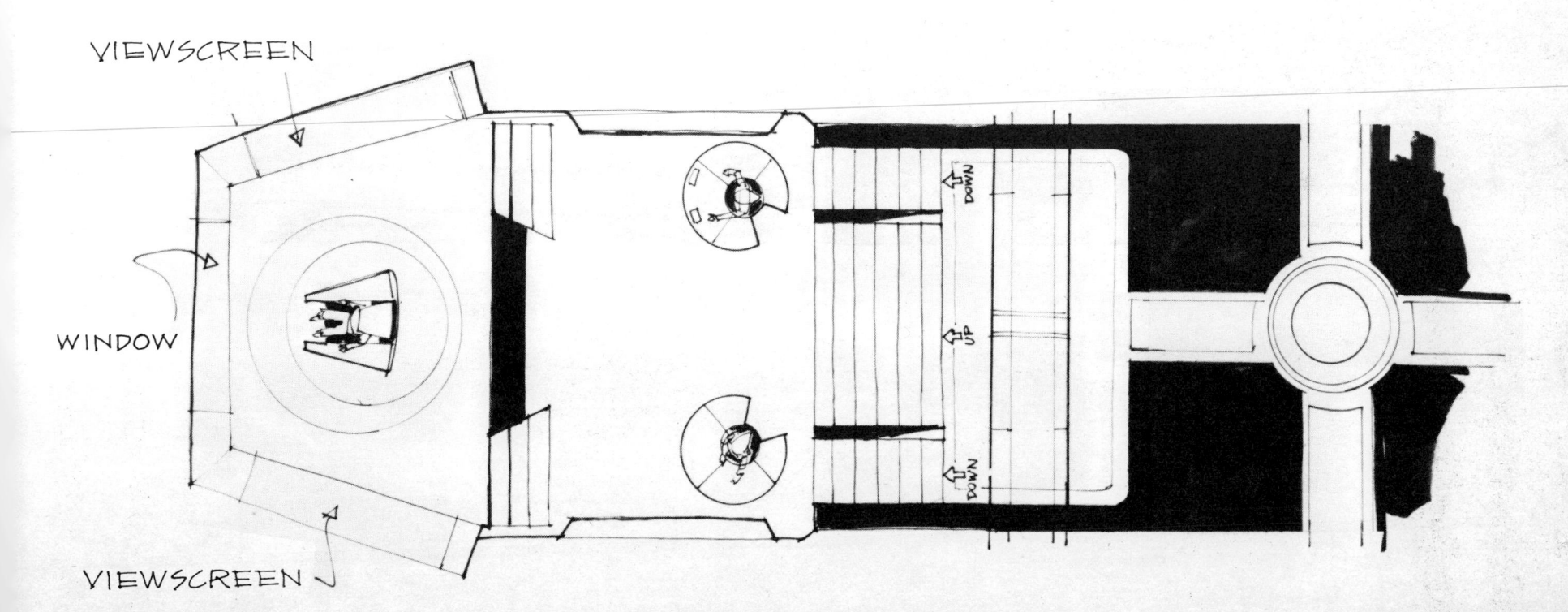

VIEWSCREEN

WINDOW

VIEWSCREEN

34 | DEATH STAR
The Throne Room

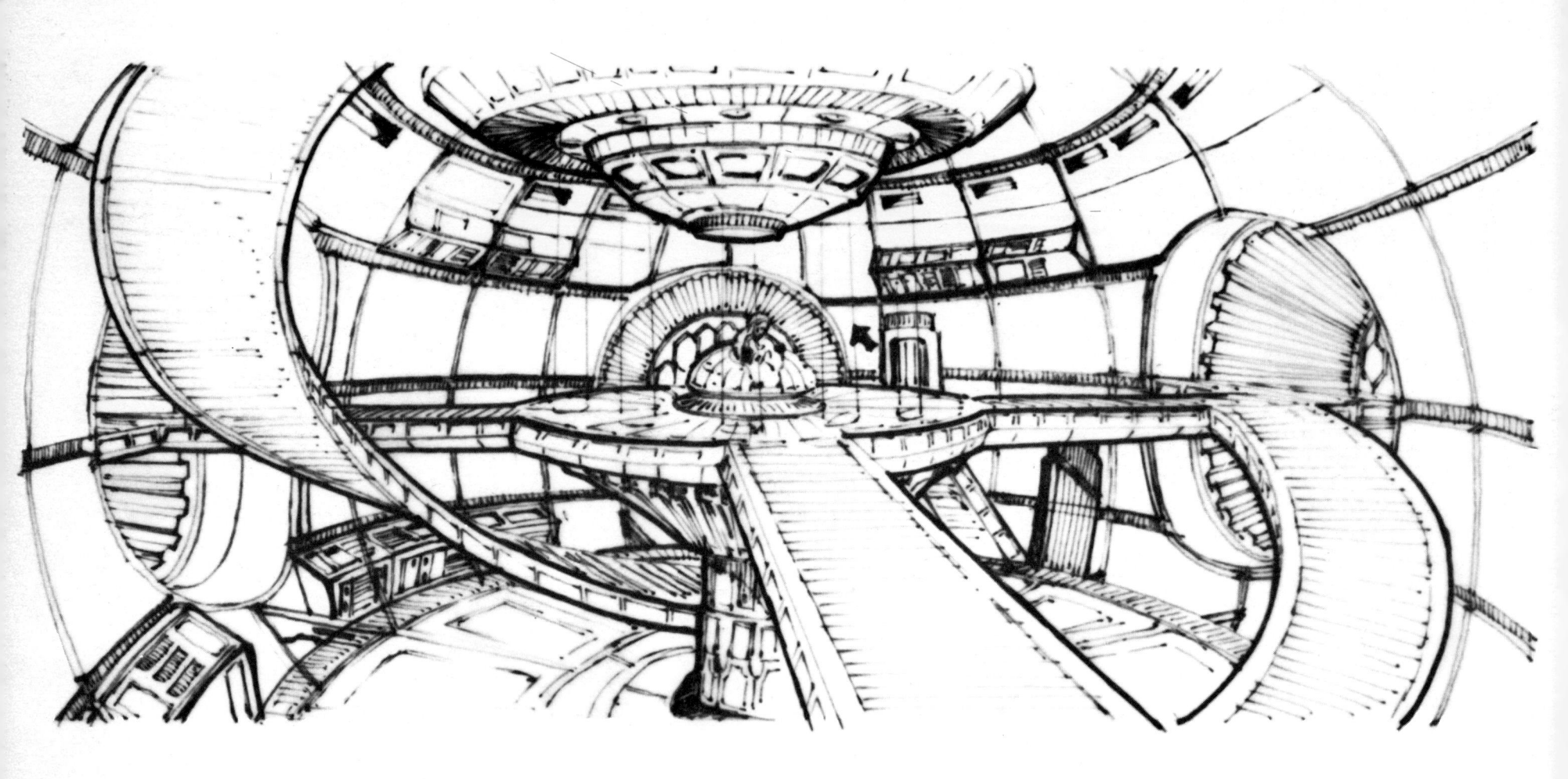

DEATH STAR
The Throne Room
85

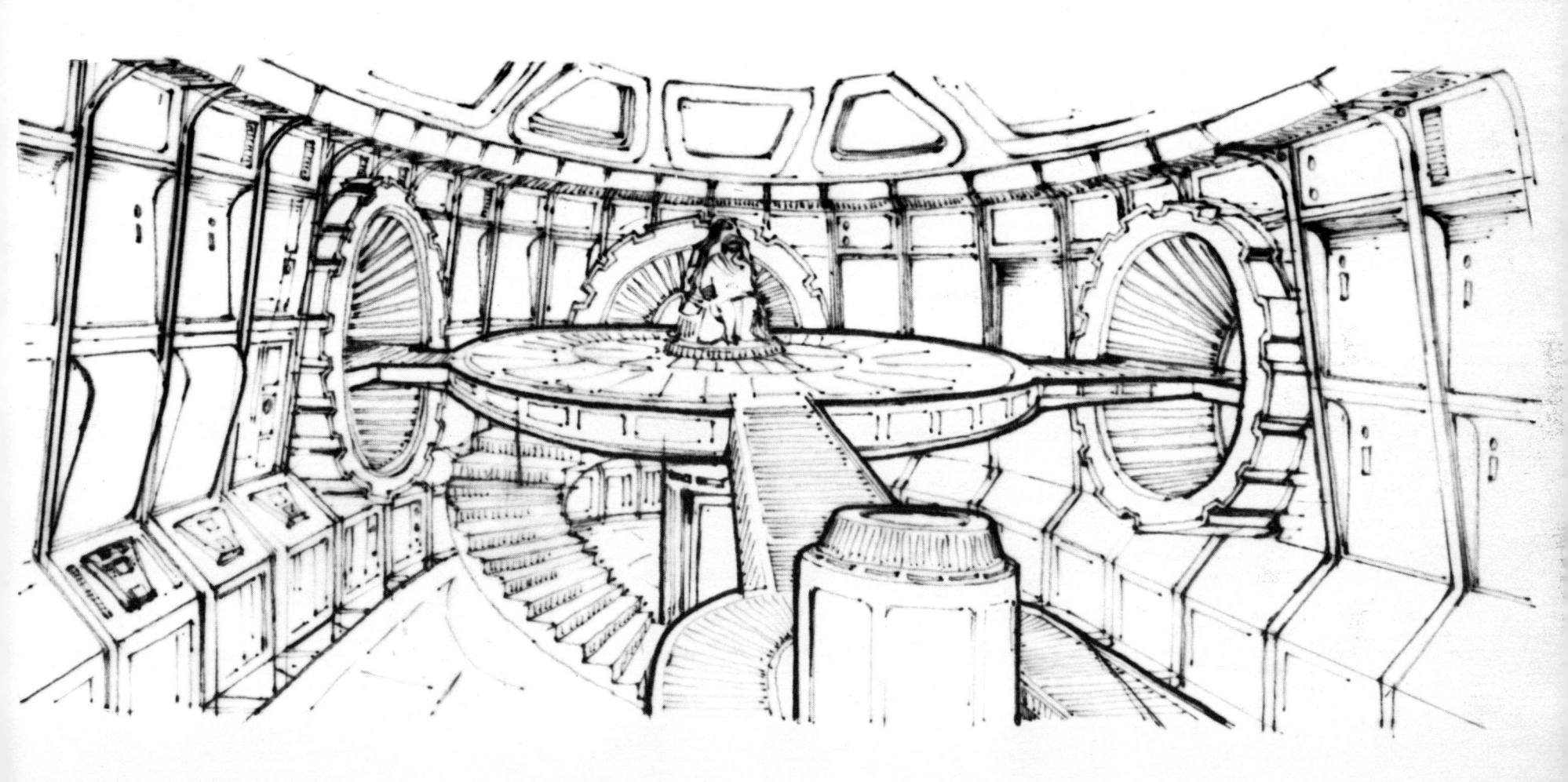

86 DEATH STAR — The Throne Room

THE EMPEROR'S OBSERVATION TOWER

REBEL SPACECRAFT

38 REBEL SPACECRAFT Cruisers

The Rebel Cruisers

The artists developed the concept of the new Rebel cruisers as more streamlined and aerodynamic looking in order to distinguish them from the more forbidding and blocklike Imperial vehicles. In these sketches the ships have a very definite, elongated, smooth shape.

MORE "BUMPS"...
ADD SEPARATE CONTROL POD W/ BRIDGE

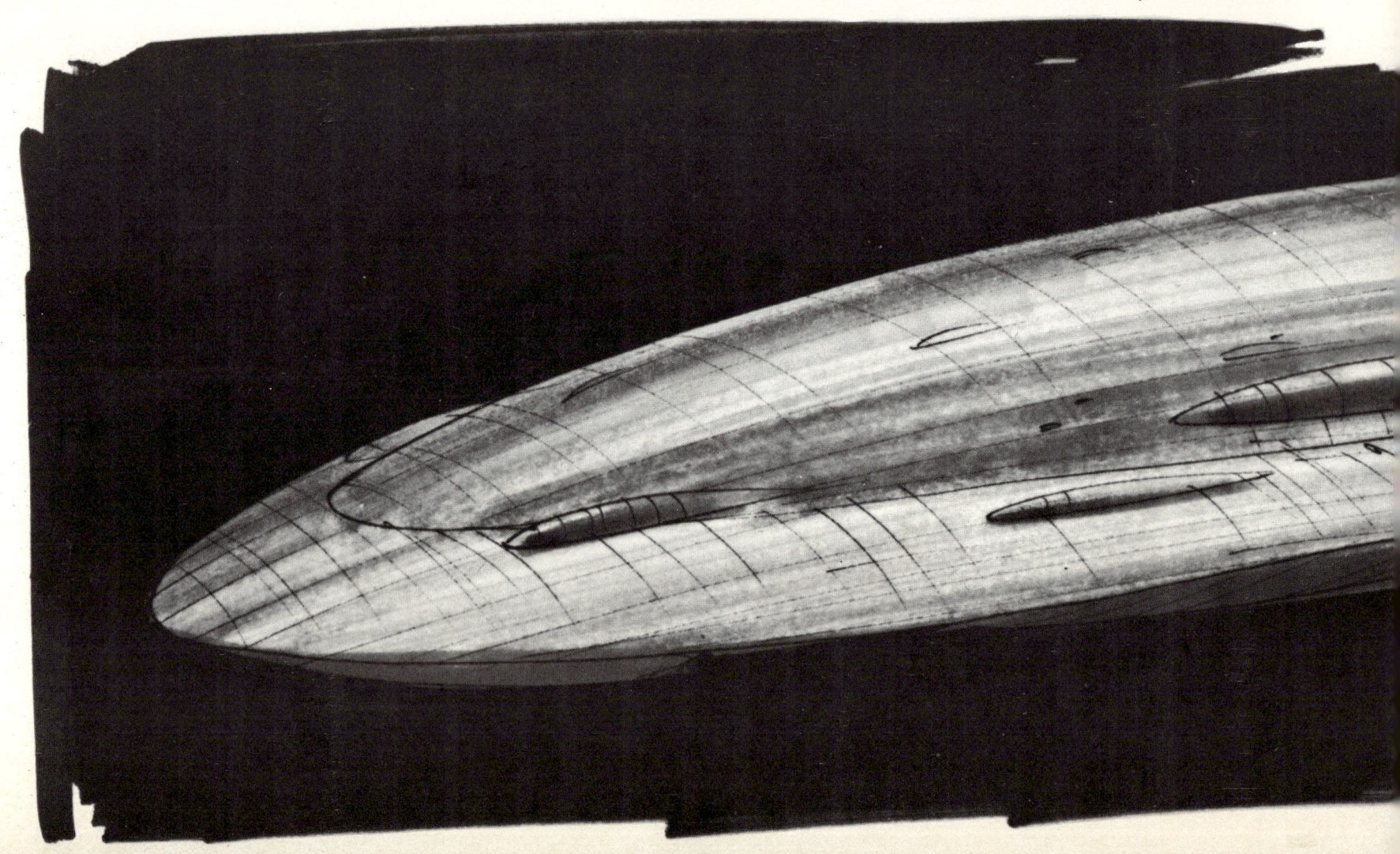

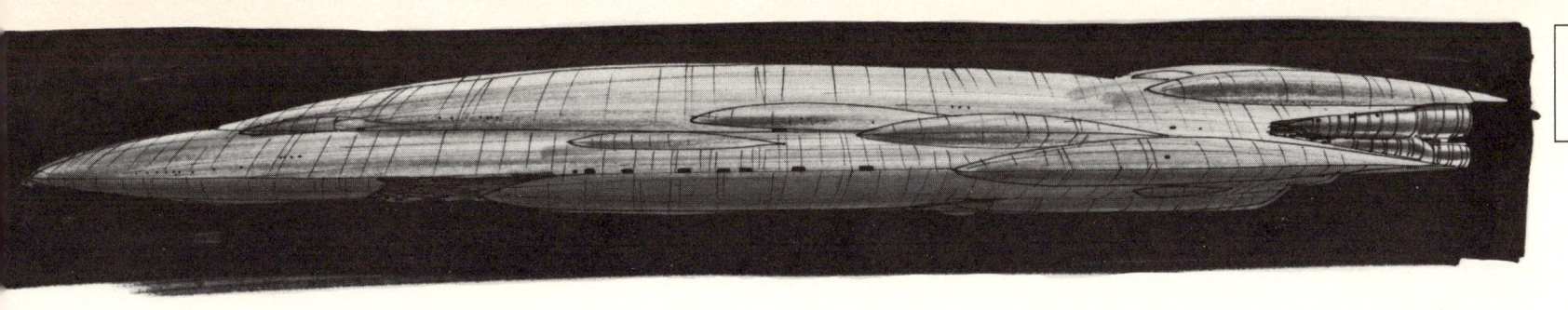

REBEL SPACECRAFT | 89
Cruisers

|— 1 MI. —|

90 | REBEL SPACECRAFT | Cruisers

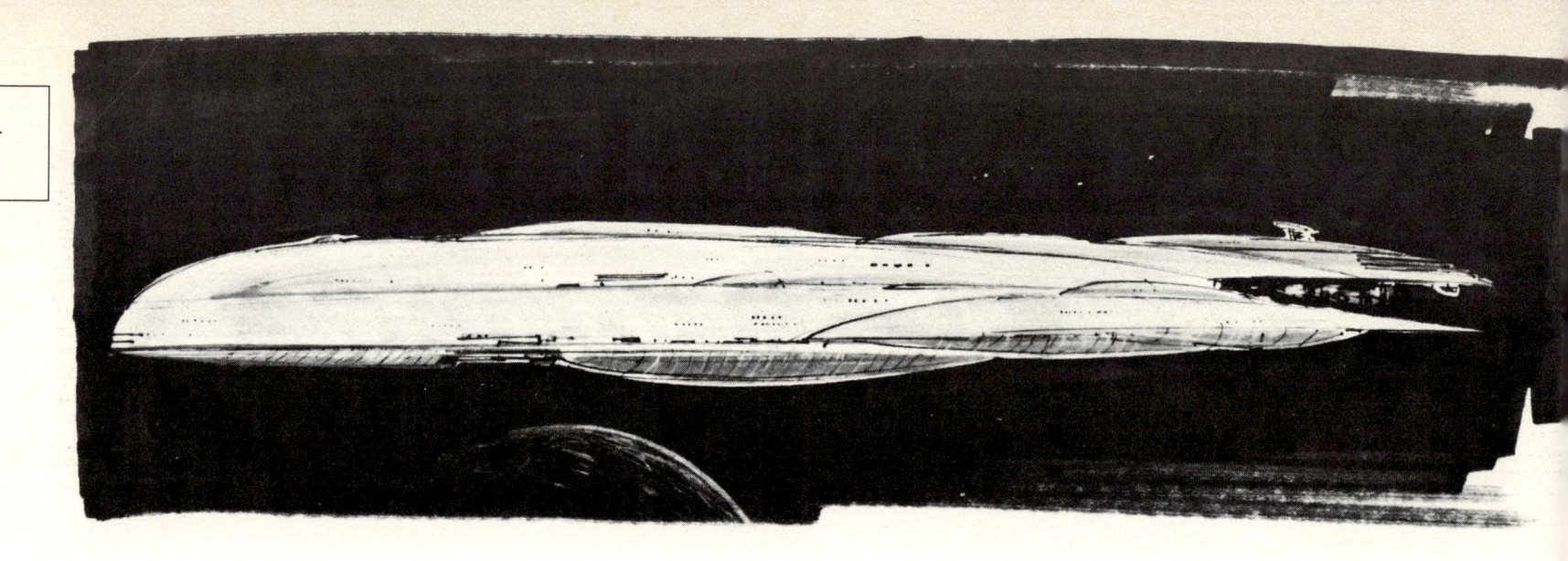

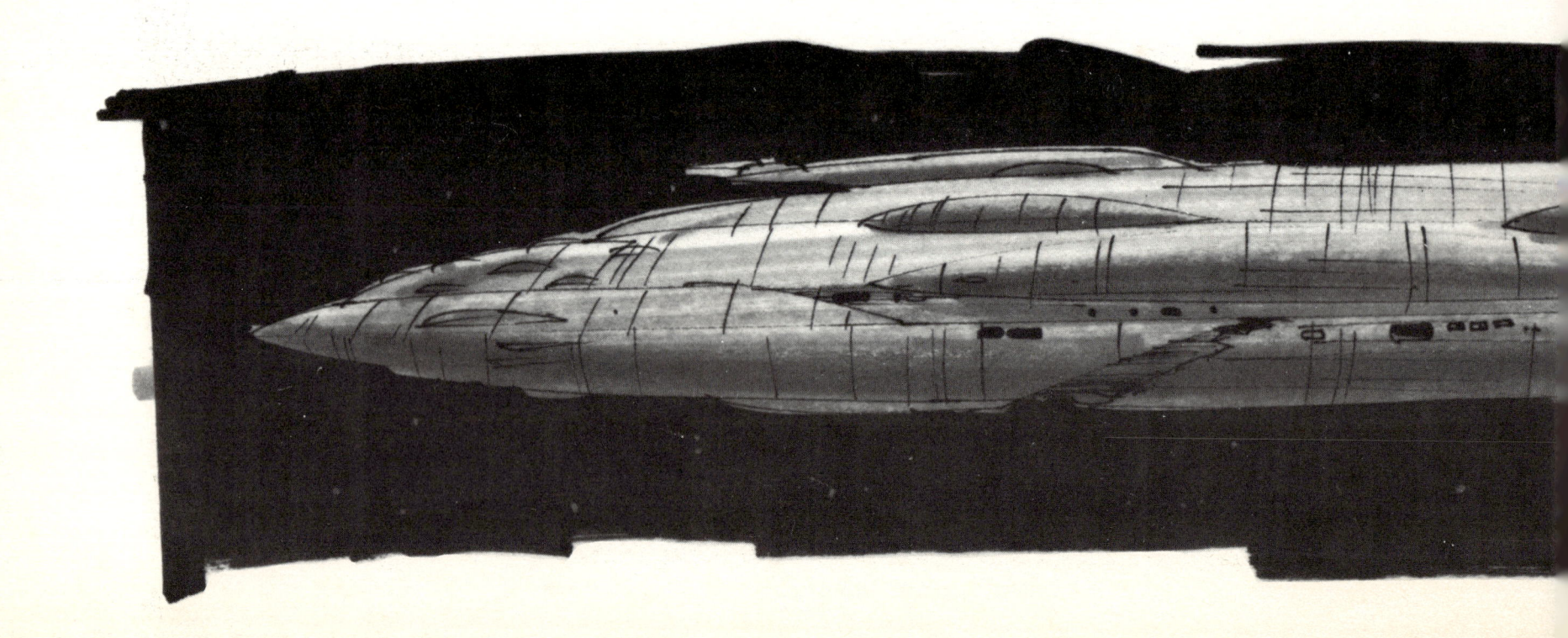

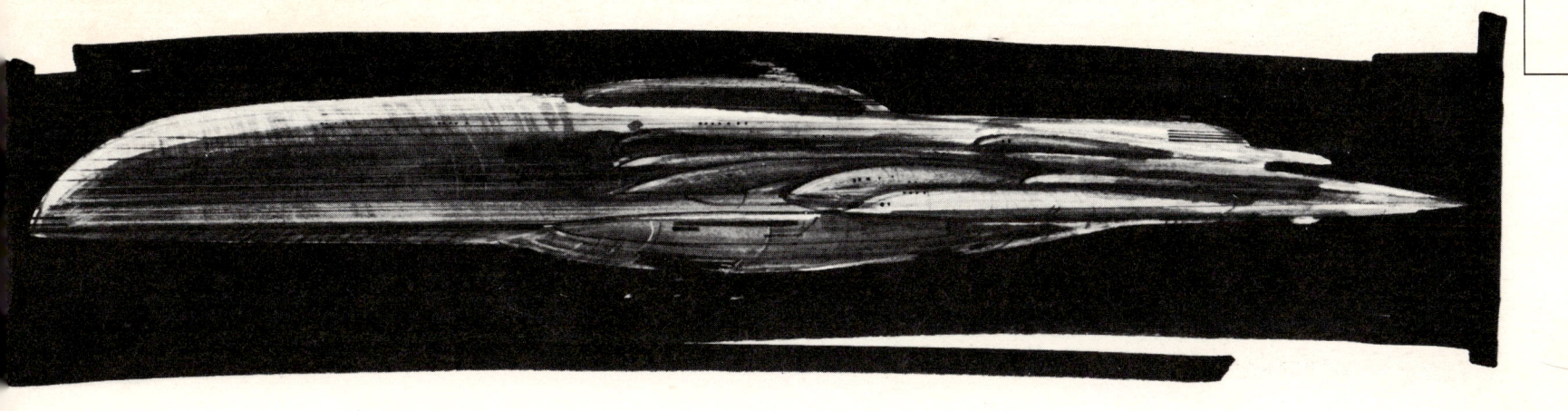

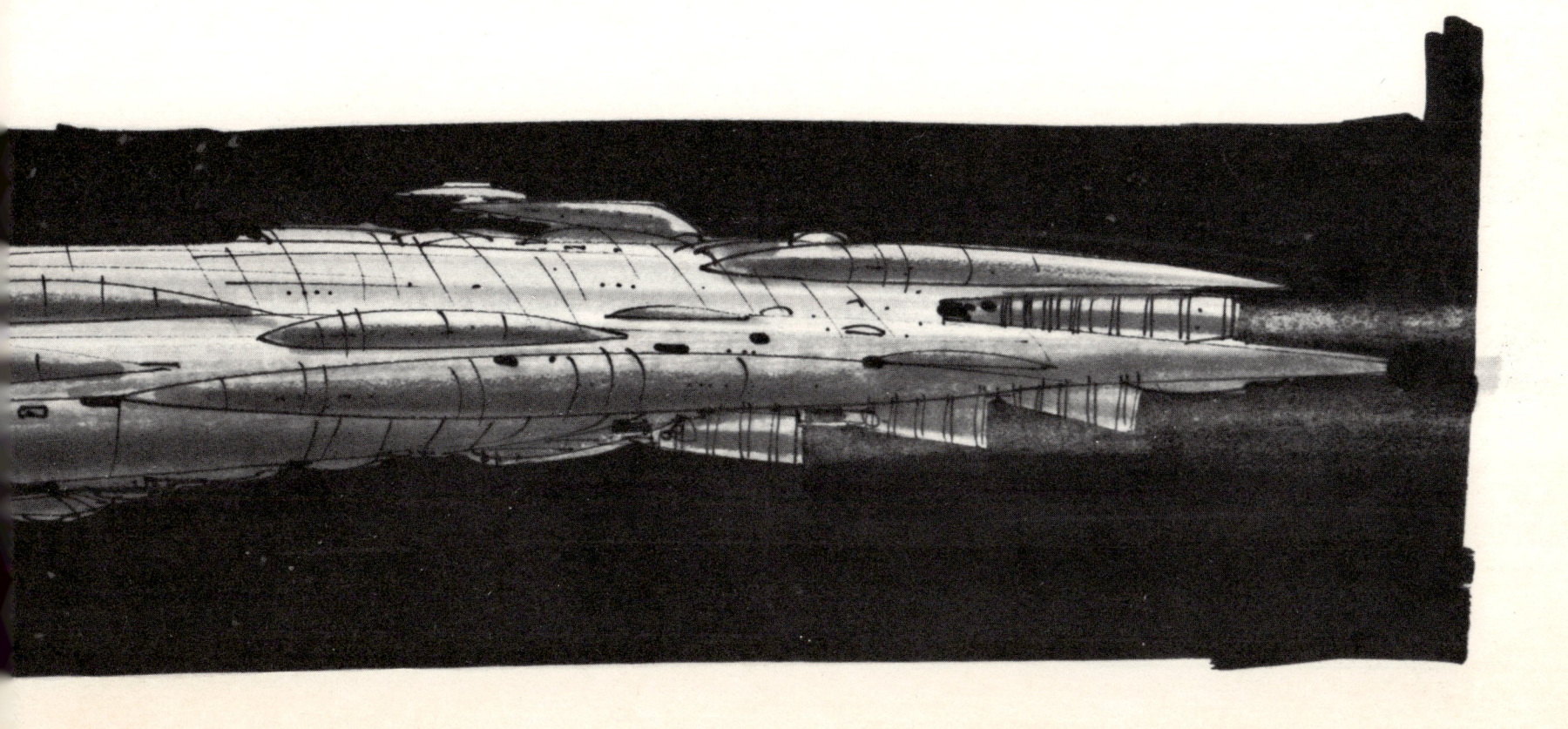

REBEL SPACECRAFT
Cruisers
91

92 | REBEL SPACECRAFT — Fighters

A-wing and B-wing Fighters

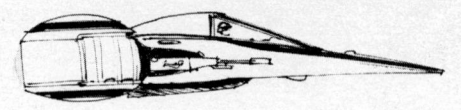

The Rebel A-wing fighter used in the attack on the Death Star bears a strong resemblance to the modified snowspeeders used on the planet Hoth. The A-wing is a compact plane designed for maximum speed and maneuverability. It has a pair of large, rear-mounted engines and a wedge-shaped nose, and is equipped with a laser cannon on each side of the streamlined wings.

The B-wing fighter, shaped like a cross, is a new Rebel combat vehicle, with a powerful cannon mounted on one of the primary wings and a pilot/copilot pod on the other. The two center wings with smaller cannons on each end of each wing fold out for battles, in for cruising. A unique feature of the B-wing is the rotating cockpit that shifts as the plane is flying so that pilot and copilot are always sitting upright.

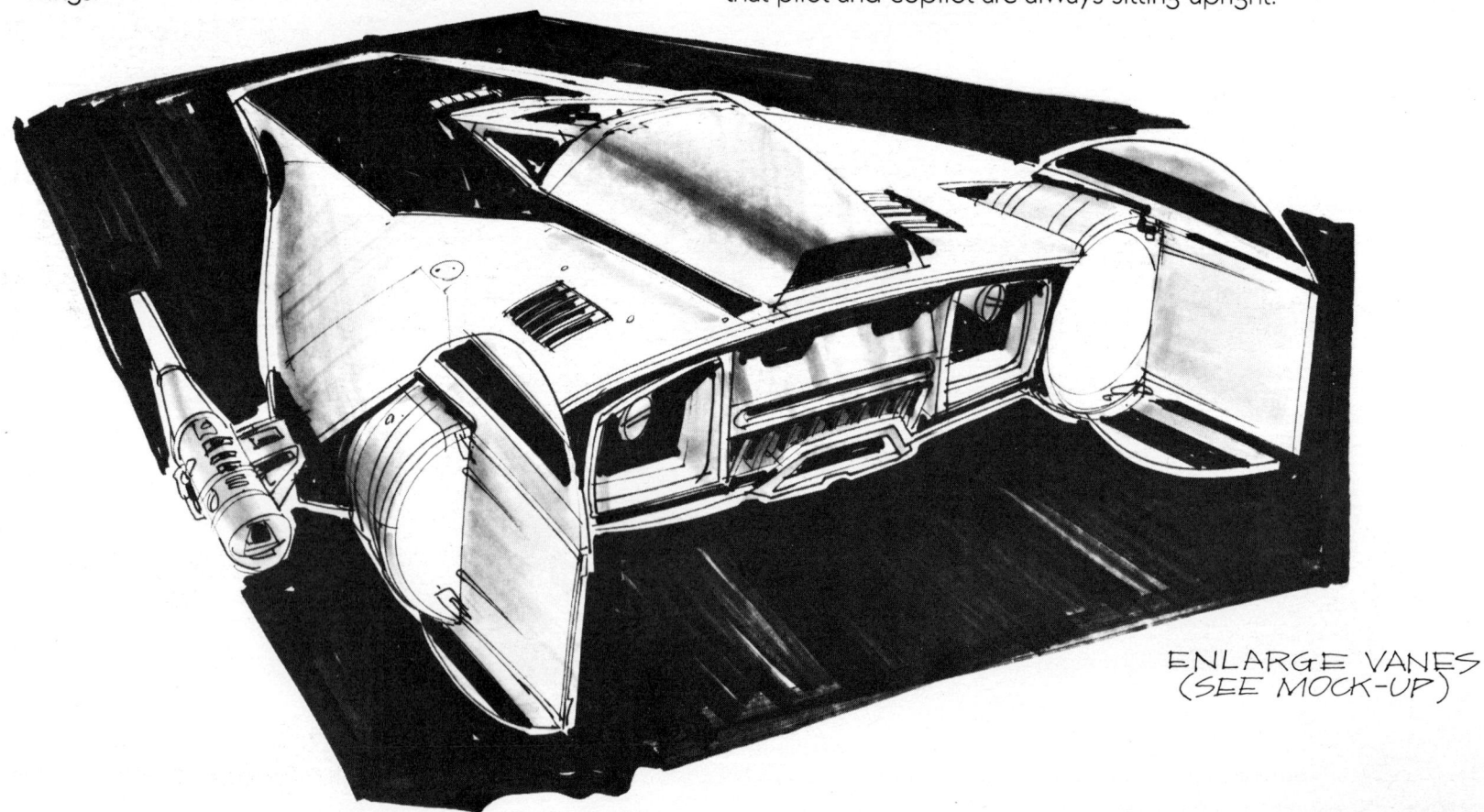

ENLARGE VANES
(SEE MOCK-UP)

REBEL SPACECRAFT 93
Fighters

| 94 | REBEL SPACECRAFT Fighters |

B-WING IS ABOUT HALF
THE SIZE OF FALCON.
NOT AS MANEUVERABLE
AS OTHER FIGHTERS

MAIN ARMAMENT

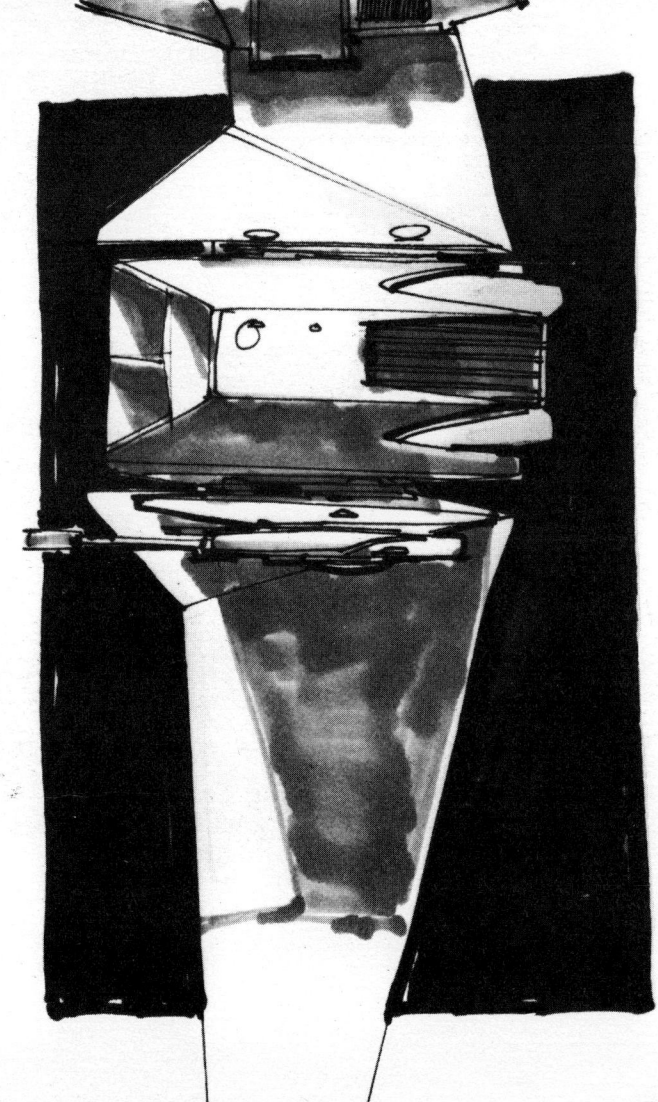

REBEL SPACECRAFT Fighters 95

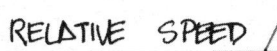

RELATIVE SPEED / MANEUVERABILITY CHART

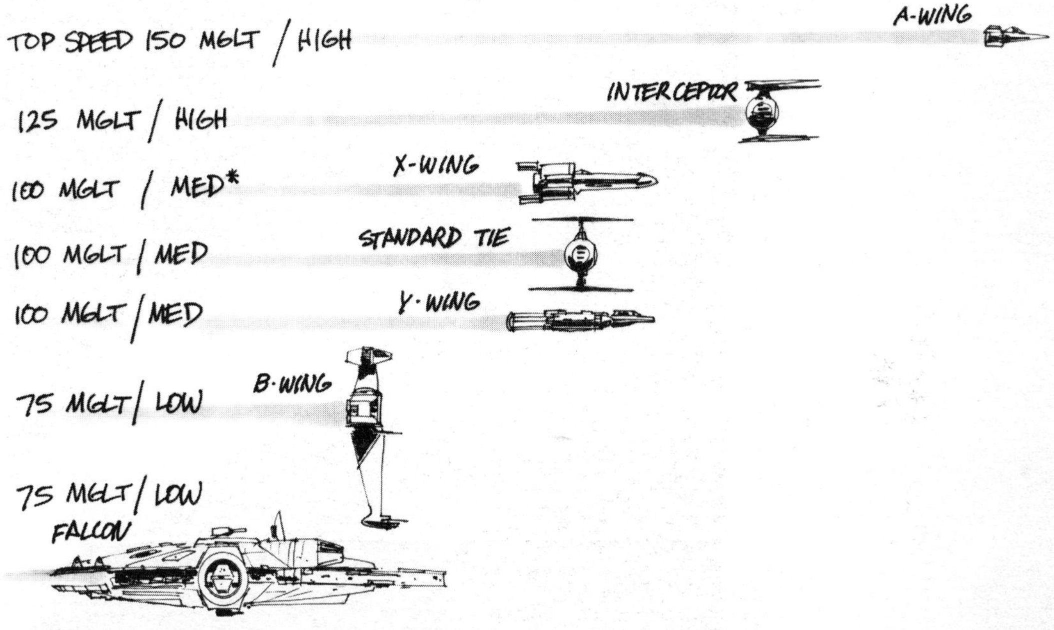

TOP SPEED 150 MGLT / HIGH — A-WING

125 MGLT / HIGH — INTERCEPTOR

100 MGLT / MED* — X-WING

100 MGLT / MED — STANDARD TIE

100 MGLT / MED — Y-WING

75 MGLT / LOW — B-WING

75 MGLT / LOW — FALCON

*MEDIUM MANEUVERABILITY = SAME AS SEEN IN STAR WARS & EMPIRE.

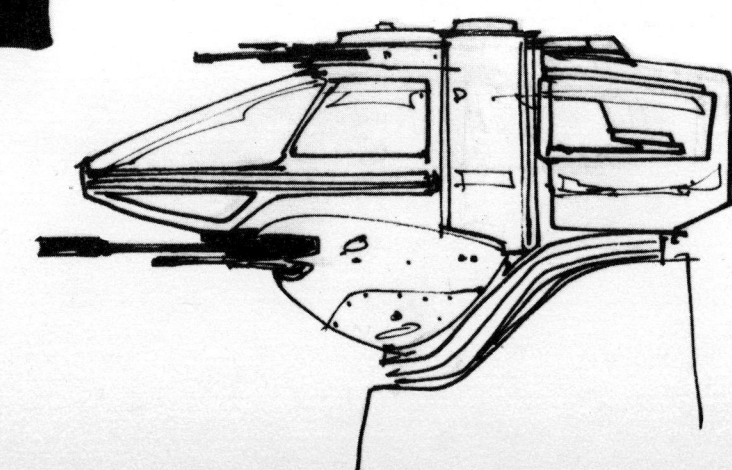

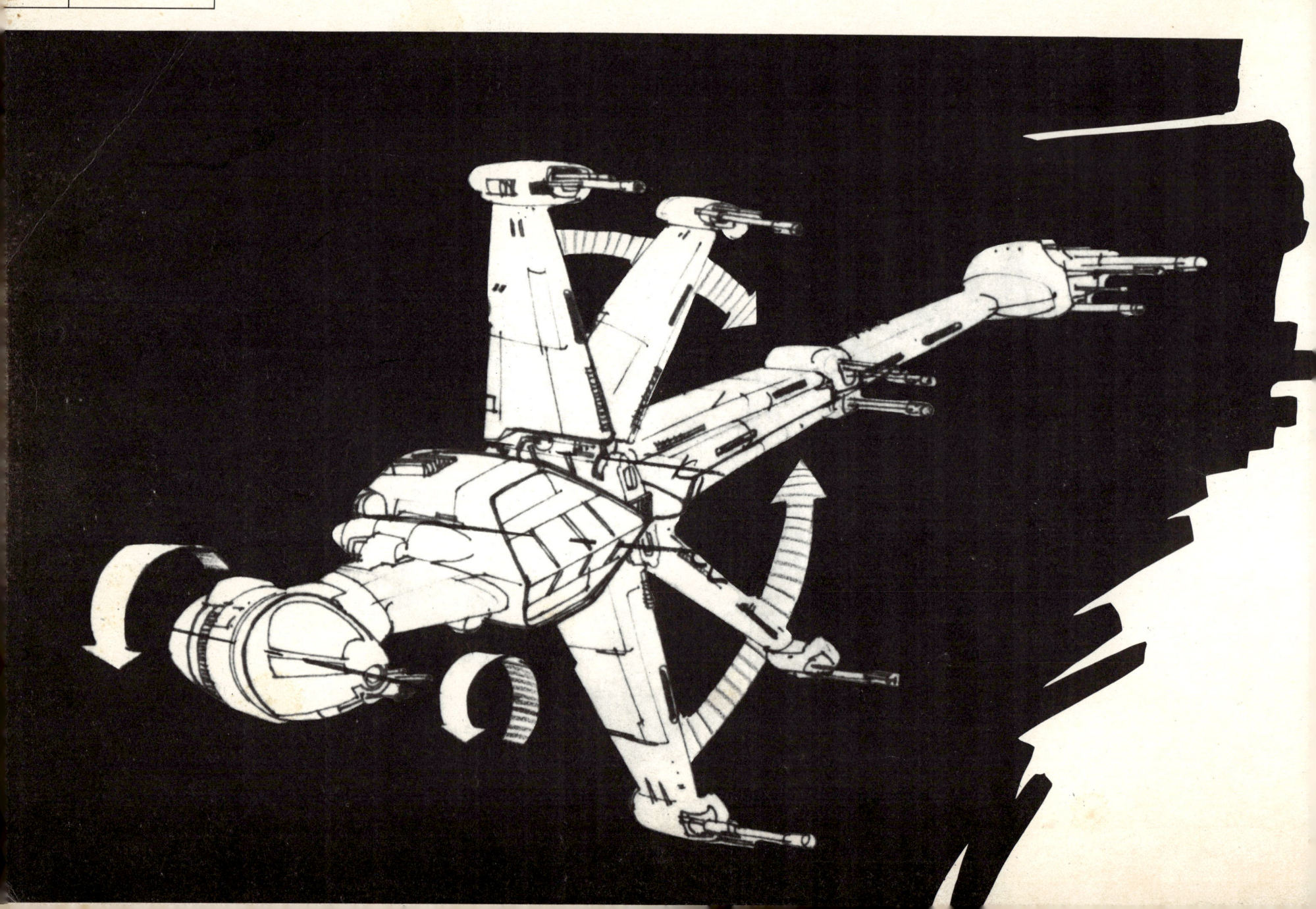

96 | REBEL SPACECRAFT | Fighters